Daughters of Destiny

a View of Biblical Heroines through the Eyes of 21st Century Women

a 40 Writer Collaboration
Volume 2

Daughters of Destiny

a View of Biblical Heroines through the Eyes of 21st Century Women

a 40 Writer Collaboration
Volume 2

Deborah G. Hunter

including 39 Contributing Writers

Daughters of Destiny, a View of Biblical Heroines through the Eyes of 21st Century Women, a 40 Writer Collaboration, Volume 2
Copyright © 2023 by Deborah G. Hunter
First Edition: December 2023

To order products, or for any other correspondence:

Hunter Entertainment Network
Colorado Springs, Colorado 80840
www.hunter-ent-net.com
Tel. (253) 906-2160
E-mail: contact@hunter-entertainment.com
Or reach us on Facebook at: Hunter Entertainment Network
"Offering God's Heart to a Dying World"

This book and all other Hunter Entertainment Network™ Hunter Heart Publishing™, and Hunter Heart Kids™ books are available at Christian bookstores and distributors worldwide.

Chief Editor: Deborah G. Hunter
Book cover design: Phil Coles Independent Design
Layout & logos: Exousia Marketing Group www.exousiamg.com

ISBN: 978-1-937741-05-1 (Paperback)
ISBN: 978-1-937741-06-8 (Hardcover)
Printed in the United States of America.

Dedication

This devotional is dedicated to the phenomenal women that have beautifully and gracefully lived their lives to please the Lord. Those that have denied themselves and died to self to pick up their own cross. Those that allowed Yeshua, Jesus the Christ, to transform their lives for His glory. If the Bible were written today, your life would be included! Thank you for loving and serving Him with your life!

Table of Contents

Introduction

The Bible was written over 2000 years ago. Over the centuries, we have come to grow extremely fond of the biblical characters we have been introduced to by some of the greatest scribes in history. Within the biblical stories of these women, we are afforded a front row seat to peer into their lives: good, bad, ugly, or indifferent. We are able to learn from their lessons, discern through their difficulties, and wield from the wisdom shared not only at the hands of the writers, but also through the breath and voice of the Spirit of the Living God. These life stories that we were graced by the Lord to experience were breathed on and inspired by the very life-giving Holy Spirit, the Ruach HaKodesh. Each and every woman mentioned in the Bible is of great significance, even if only her name is written.

God speaks nothing haphazardly. Every word, and yes, every name spoken, reflects and reveals something of great importance to our heavenly Father. As you journey through this devotional, *Daughters of Destiny, a View of Biblical Heroines through the Eyes of 21st Century Women*, *Volume 2*, utilize your heavenly imagination and travel back throughout biblical times to get to know these amazing women of the Bible. Read, study, and meditate upon their lives so you are able to understand their significance of being included, and how their lives tie into the birth, life, death, burial, and resurrection of our Lord and Savior, the Messiah, Jesus the Christ. Also, witness how ordinary, yet profound, women of the 21st Century parallel their lives to their biblical heroines.

Deborah G. Hunter

"And they overcame him by the blood of the Lamb and by the word of their testimony, and they did not love their lives to the death" Revelation 12:11.

Your testimony is one of the most powerful evangelistic tools you can possess! As you read these transparent and compelling stories, allow the Spirit of God to ignite His fire within you to go into all the world to share with others what He has done for you! You are a *Daughter of Destiny!*

Hannah

Deborah G. Hunter, *49 years old*

"So it came to pass in the process of time that Hannah conceived and bore a son, and called his name Samuel, saying, "Because I have asked for him from the Lord." 1 Samuel 1:20

At the age of nineteen, I was diagnosed with cervical cancer. After going through surgery, I was told that I would never be able to have children. This prognosis from the doctors sent me into great depression at the thought that I would never be able to hear the word, "Mommy" from my children. Though I was still a young woman and not married, my heart's desire was to one day, birth my own children. I am confident that this cancer was a result of an abortion three years prior. Time went on and at the age of twenty-one, my appendix almost ruptured and I was rushed into emergency surgery. Upon waking up, I was told that I had a cyst the size of a grapefruit resting on my ovary. My appendectomy was not the result of a failed appendix, but a consequence of a large cyst pushing against my appendix, which was minutes from rupturing. I was informed, once again, that the damage to my right ovary would hinder me from ever having children of my own. I was faced with the reality that my sin had very real consequences.

"The labor of the righteous leads to life, The wages of the wicked to sin" Proverbs 10:16, NKJV.

I was saved at the age of twelve. I gave my life to the Lord in Vacation Bible School in 1986 on the heels of learning my father was diagnosed with terminal lung cancer, along with eight massive brain tumors. I knew *of* the Lord, but did not know Him intimately. So, receiving these two devastating reports did not come with immediate faith, especially since my father had succumbed to his own cancer diagnoses. This second "hit," along with losing my father at such a young age, caused a hardening of sorts in my heart. After his death, I lost it and went into great rebellion. I became very promiscuous and got pregnant at a young age, resulting in me aborting my first child. I experienced tremendous grief at what I had done; the guilt remained with me for years. Each time I received the doctor's report that I would never have children, I beat myself up with guilt and shame, accepting my "lot" in life due to my sin.

"The thief does not come except to steal, and to kill, and to destroy. I have come that they may have life, and that they may have it more abundantly" John 10:10, NKJV.

My sister that I was saved with at the age of twelve, she fourteen, Sandi, was now serving the Lord faithfully and growing exponentially in her faith. Her assignment at this time in my life was leading me back to Christ, though I fought it at every turn. I am not sure if I was angry with God or that my faith was simply shattered due to so much loss in my life at that time. Nevertheless, I believe wholeheartedly that her prayers, her love for me, and her willingness to keep witnessing to me softened my heart and led me back to my first love.

I met my husband a year later and I became pregnant with my first child and at the age of twenty-two, my beautiful baby girl entered the world. We named her Jade Aaliyah. She was such an absolute joy to my life. I did not know I could ever love someone so much, but God revealed His Glory to me and my faith began to grow. It took a lot of healing and forgiving of myself for taking the life of my unborn child at the age of sixteen. I was led to an organization called *The National Memorial for the Unborn* where I could create a memorial for my unborn son. Yes, God revealed to me I conceived a son. During my healing process, and creating his memorial, my final healing came by naming him. His name, Andrew. Today, he would be thirty-three years old. There were many days and nights that I wept deeply for him. I know now I will meet him in Heaven one day.

"The Lord has heard my weeping. The Lord has heard my cry for mercy; the Lord accepts my prayer" Psalm 6:6, NIV.

Hannah was a barren woman. The Word of God grants us a glimpse into the life of this faithful woman of God. She was one of two wives of Elkanah, the other being Peninnah. Peninnah was able to birth children and consistently provoked Hannah because she was the barren wife. Hannah grieved deeply that she could not conceive children for Elkanah who loved her dearly. The Bible states that it was the Lord who had closed her womb. We are not fully privy of the reason, but we understand all throughout Scripture and even in our own lives that there is a reason for everything under the sun, and there are always lessons to learn in the waiting. It states that she went up to the Temple year after year, offering sacrifices to the Lord weeping bitterly and not eating. Can you imagine the thoughts running through Hannah's mind? Did she grow angry with God? Was her faith shattered due to the "lot" she had been granted in life? Was she angry with her husband, Elkanah, for diminishing her feelings of barrenness by questioning that he was not enough by saying to her, *"Hannah, why do you weep? Why do you not eat? And why is your heart grieved? Am I not better to you than ten sons,"* 1 Samuel 1:8, NKJV. Well, we are afforded the answer in Scripture. Though Hannah grieved deeply her barren womb, she loved her husband and served him faithfully and loved the Lord deeply, honoring Him year after year with the sacrifices of her tears and offerings unto Him despite her *affliction*.

"So Hannah arose after they had finished eating and drinking in Shiloh. Now Eli the priest was sitting on the seat by the doorpost of the tabernacle of the Lord. And she was in bitterness of soul, and prayed to the Lord and wept in anguish. Then she made a vow and said, "O Lord of hosts, if You will indeed look on the affliction of Your maidservant and remember me, and not forget Your maidservant, but will give Your maidservant a male child, then I will give him to the Lord all the days of his life, and no razor shall come upon his head" 1 Samuel 1:9-11, NKJV.

There was some sort of affliction in Hannah's body hindering her from conceiving a child. Even in great bitterness in her soul, weeping, and anguish, Hannah prayed faithfully to the Lord making a vow to Him. She went on further to say that *"no razor shall come upon his head"*. This vow is symbolic of the Nazarite vow of honor which revealed complete submission and surrender to God one's life for service.

Six years after the birth of my first child, my husband and I conceived again. In the seventh month of my pregnancy, we had planned a baby shower and on the day of the shower was my first ultrasound appointment. We were so excited to find out if we were having a boy or another girl. The night before the ultrasound, I had, by far, the most divinely led dream of my entire life. In the dream, I was standing in my kitchen making my daughter lunch. All of a sudden, a blinding light burst through my kitchen window and I began to hear children laughing and playing outside. I walked to my front door and opened it, and looked over into the parking lot and there were children everywhere, only it wasn't a parking lot, but what looked like a garden. There was a *man* standing in the midst of the children and He glanced over at me. I could not contain my emotions, and just began weeping. I was somehow drawn, or taken over, to Him, and I fell to my knees. He placed His hand on my chin and lifted my head up to Him. I was not able to see His face as the light was so bright, but His voice was so calm yet so clear. These were the words He spoke to me, *"Daughter, because you have been faithful to Me, I have given you and your husband a son. You will call him Elijah."*

The peace that flooded my entire being is inexplicable, even to this day. I awakened and could not even wait for my husband to wake up, so I woke him up! I shared the dream with him and told him that I was cancelling our ultrasound appointment, because God had already revealed that we were, indeed, having a son and that we would name him Elijah. That morning, I knelt and prayed to my Father in Heaven, thanking Him in advance for our son. I knew from the dream that my first son was with Him in Glory and that He had forgiven me. My grief and shame was washed away by His love and replaced with absolute joy.

"And Hannah prayed and said: "My heart rejoices in the Lord; My horn is exalted in the Lord. I smile at my enemies, Because I rejoice in Your salvation" 1 Samuel 2:1, NKJV.

HANNAH

Hannah received a son and called him Samuel saying, *"Because I have asked for him from the Lord."* God honored my heartfelt repentance and gave me a son, calling him Elijah. He would be a prophetic promise, not only to me, but also to my husband. Father revealed to me Malachi 4 and the Spirit of Elijah, the Prophet, that would bring the hearts of the fathers to the children, and the hearts of the children to their fathers. The enemy knew this, as well. The day I went into labor with Elijah, he flipped and the umbilical cord wrapped around his neck. His heart rate began to drop drastically. I could see the sheer fear on the nurses faces and I looked up at the heart monitor and saw it dropping fast. Immediately, Holy Spirit came upon me. I went into warfare for my son. I began to give God back His Word, His Promise, and His Divine Interruption of my sleep, the heavenly encounter and proclamation of Elijah's birth. He is not a man that He should lie nor the son of man that He should repent. If He said it, He would surely perform it! I began praying in the Spirit and worshiping my Father in Heaven. Suddenly, I felt a flip on the inside. Elijah's heart rate began to climb and I could see the relief not only on the nurses faces, but also my husband's. He was right there praying and interceding with me for our precious son! Moments later, my husband was able to deliver and receive his son into the world.

Hannah honored her vow to the Lord and after Samuel was weaned, she took him up to the Temple and gave him to the service of God. After years and years of barrenness, unexplainable grief, shame, and bitterness of soul, Hannah gave up her son to God. What honor! What reverence! What faithfulness!!! I, too, made a vow to the Lord regarding my son. I have watched and listened closely to the "divine whispers of Heaven" concerning his life. The Lord visited me again in my dreams in 2019, and showed me His plans for Elijah. Part one has already been fulfilled! Stay tuned for Part two!

"Do you still believe Me," says the Lord? Trust Him and serve Him even in your weeping, even in your waiting. Not one tear will go uncaught. Not one prayer will go unanswered. He is El Roi, the God who sees! He saw Hannah. He saw me. He sees you!

Deborah

Jacqueline J. Bott, *73 years old*

"Now Deborah, a prophetess, the wife of Lapidoth, was judging Israel at that time." Judges 4:4

Everyday Warrior. There have been a number of books written about the Prophet Deborah and her anointing. How she was not only a prophet, but a judge, poet, singer, songwriter, and warrior. She achieved a great victory and saved her people against an evil adversary. You can find her story in Judges 4 and 5 in the Bible. Deborah was successful because she sought guidance from the Lord in all matters. She was a just woman both wise and humble.

"Now Deborah, a prophetess, the wife of Lapidoth, was judging Israel at that time. And she would sit under the palm tree of Deborah between Ramah and Bethel in the mountains of Ephraim. And the children of Israel came up to her for judgment" Judges 4:4-5, NKJV.

This is exactly the type of women the Lord is calling today to do battle for Him. Do not be fooled by the enemy and think that you haven't any power, because you do. The Lord above has no limits and will equip you through His Word. Not only that, but you also have tools of protection in His Word. You can find these tools in Ephesians 6:10-18.

"Finally, my brethren, be strong in the Lord and in the power of His might. Put on the whole armor of God, that you may be able to stand against the wiles of the devil. For we do not wrestle against flesh and blood, but against principalities, against powers, against the rulers of the darkness of this age, against spiritual hosts of wickedness in the heavenly places. Therefore take up the whole armor of God, that you may be able to withstand in the evil day, and having done all, to stand. Stand therefore, having girded your waist with truth, having put on the breastplate of righteousness, and having shod your feet with the preparation of the gospel of peace; above all, taking the shield of faith with which you will be able to quench all the fiery darts of the wicked one. And take the helmet of salvation, and the sword of the Spirit, which is the word of God; praying always with all prayer and supplication in the Spirit, being watchful to this end with all perseverance and supplication for all the saints—" NKJV.

If you haven't realized it yet, we are at war! In the natural, as well as spiritual. This means, all hands on deck. Every man, woman, and child that has accepted the Lord into their hearts is an everyday warrior. I believe that women can tap into the attributes of Deborah and do mighty things in the spirit realm as well as the natural. Women can be fierce warriors for their families and fight against the chaos going on around them.

"Then she sent and called for Barak the son of Abinoam from Kedesh in Naphtali, and said to him, "Has not the Lord God of Israel commanded, 'Go and deploy troops at Mount Tabor; take with you ten thousand men of the sons of Naphtali and of the sons of Zebulun; and against you I will deploy Sisera, the commander of Jabin's army, with his chariots and his multitude at the River Kishon; and I will deliver him into your hand'?" Judges 4:6-7, NKJV.

God anointed Deborah not only as a judge and a fierce warrior, but He commissioned her as a prophet to prophesy to Barak to organize his troops in preparation to battle Sisera, the commander of Jabin's army, and his men. Women in these last days must be bold and courageous in their calling as Deborah was and lift up their voices to speak all that the Lord has commanded them to speak. In her confidence and obedience,

DEBORAH

Deborah won the trust, approval, and admiration of Barak, a military commander. Women of God, there are places of great power and authority that God desires to send you forth into in order to shift atmospheres. But just as we see in the attributes of Deborah, not only was she wise, but she was also humble. She understood authority both in the natural and the spiritual. She was not only under the authority of her natural head, her husband, Lapidoth, and under the spiritual authority of her God, but Deborah also understood the authority of Barak and what God was calling him to do. She did not usurp authority and try to go and win this battle herself. No! Her assignment was to prophesy into this man's life, so he could fulfill his earthly calling. What honor, what power, what authority! Listen to the words of Barak to Deborah:

"And Barak said to her, "If you will go with me, then I will go; but if you will not go with me, I will not go!" Judges 4:8, NKJV.

Deborah's boldness opened the door to reciprocal honor as Barak recognized the authority *and* the anointing on her life. Women of God, the ultimate desire of God is for absolute unity amongst the Body of Christ; man, woman, and child walking alongside one another in their designed and assigned positions for the Glory of God. When this is witnessed in its fullness, the Bible declares the blessing over it!

"Behold, how good and how pleasant it is
For brethren to dwell together in unity!
It is like the precious oil upon the head,
Running down on the beard,
The beard of Aaron,
Running down on the edge of his garments.
It is like the dew of Hermon,
Descending upon the mountains of Zion;
For there the Lord commanded the blessing—
Life forevermore." Psalm 133:1-3, NKJV

Deborah wasn't vying for Barak's position, and Barak was not coveting Deborah's calling. They both understood the unique gifting, assignment, and calling on one another's life and joined together to fulfill God's divine command. In doing so, they made way for another that God would ultimately use to defeat Sisera, the commander of Jabin's army. Her name… yes, a woman… Jael.

Deborah declared to Barak when asked to go with him to battle,

"So she said, "I will surely go with you; nevertheless there will be no glory for you in the journey you are taking, for the Lord will sell Sisera into the hand of a woman" Judges 4:9.

Once again, Barak received the voice of God through the Prophet Deborah whom God had revealed to beforehand that a woman, Jael, would be the one used to kill Sisera. He, in turn, humbled himself and went forth into battle with Deborah and ultimately, Jael. What unity! And what did God do? He commanded the blessing over a nation! What could we, as the Body of Christ today, accomplish for the Glory of God Almighty if we would simply humble ourselves, honor the gifts, assignments, and calling of our brothers and sisters in Christ, and join together to fulfill His divine purposes in the Earth?

Deborah could be trusted. She understood the multifaceted plan of God because she spent time in His presence. Intimacy was her banner and her shield. Her desire was to fulfill His glorious will, not her own. Her obedience to His Voice led to so many others fulfilling their own God-given assignments in this world in her time, and even still to this day. Deborah's voice is yet prophesying!

Just like Deborah, seek the Lord in all matters and see what happens. The Lord will meet you where you are at! Become the warrior, prophet, poet, singer, songwriter, mother, grandmother, great-grandmother, daughter, sister, wife, and friend that He has called you to be.

BECOME THAT EVERYDAY WARRIOR!

Ruth

Alyssa Simone Floyd, *40 years old*

"But Ruth replied, "Don't ask me to leave you and turn back. Wherever you go, I will go; wherever you live, I will live. Your people will be my people, and your God will be my God." Ruth 1:16

Ruth's story starts with unfortunate events. Her father-in-law dies and eventually, her husband and brother-in-law die also. She is left alone with her mother-in-law Naomi and sister-in-law Orpah. She had the opportunity to return to her people instead of continuing within a family that experienced so much loss.

Ruth was best known for her loyalty to Naomi who was ultimately loyal to her God. Ruth's loyalty helped her connect to her Kingsman redeemer, the one who would redeem her and her family. He was the one that she would marry and eventually fulfill the purpose for her generation. What Ruth did not know from the one decision that she would make to stay with her mother-in-law was that it would change the direction of her life and she would be in the family line of Jesus because of her obedience.

Loyalty is often missing from our generation, especially when things don't go how we planned them to go. God forbid that there is grief, disloyalty, or anything that causes us to be in an uncomfortable situation. Loyalty is usually the first thing to go in order to stay in what people may think is a "safe place". Ruth decided that loyalty to her mother-in-law would be the safest place for her. This was also the will of God for her life.

Growing up in a Christian home, I would hear that being in the will of God is the safest place that you can be. Staying inside of the will of God can look like giving up things, saying no when it's unpopular, and putting a stop to situations that we think would fulfill us. Personally, in my young adult years, I had to learn what loyalty to the Holy Spirit was and what it was not. This was during a time when it was not acceptable and not exciting to be loyal to anything that was not self-serving. Young adults at that time were self-seeking, selfish, only looking out for themselves, and just outright rebellious.

An experience with the Holy Spirit wrecked my life in the best way at the age of seventeen and set me on the path to true loyalty. I thank God for the baptism of the Holy Spirit where I received the power to live a life that was God-ordained. That encounter made me never want to leave this newfound life. Just like Ruth, I was allowed to follow in the path of the Lord (her Naomi), or to go back to what I knew, and what was popular at the time (Ruth's and Orpah's old life). I had the decision to make which just like Ruth, would put me on the path to loving God and being right smack in the middle of His will. I chose to remain loyal to God whom I loved. I did not know what that life would look like. I had no immediate direction as to what my life would look like in the future and to be honest, I didn't know what true happiness, or what the world deemed as happy, would look like for me. I was leaving a life that looked like fun, leaving friends behind and leaving the "normal" college life behind for the "spiritual life" that was reserved for the older generation.

I can't help but compare my experience to Ruth's life. Even though Ruth experienced loss, she gained a trusted confidant in her mother-in-law, Naomi. I experienced a lot of loss in friendships that did not want what I wanted and experienced depression, at times, because of loss yet I gained a trusted friend in the Holy Spirit. The beautiful thing about having a relationship with the Holy Spirit is that His relationship will sustain you and put you in a place where your heart can be safe. The

RUTH

Bible says in the Book of John that as Jesus was leaving and promising the Holy Spirit that He would be our helper, our advocate, our comforter and the list goes on. John 14:16-18 says this: *"And I will ask the Father, and He will give you another Helper (Comforter, Advocate, Intercessor —Counselor, Strengthener, Standby), to be with you forever—the Spirit of Truth, whom the world cannot receive [and take to its heart] because it does not see Him or know Him, but you know Him because He (the Holy Spirit) remains with you continually and will be in you. "I will not leave you as orphans [comfortless, bereaved, and helpless]; I will come [back] to you."*

As I read the book of Ruth, I see how Ruth's loyalty and obedience to Naomi and God take her down a road of favor and blessings. Ruth may have thought that her only purpose for the remainder of her life was to serve her mother-in-law, but she caught the favor of someone that could redeem her and bless her and her legacy. God doesn't always show us what our obedience and loyalty will do, but trusting in the path of the unknown oftentimes brings rewards. Just like Ruth was led, The Holy Spirit will lead and guide us.

"Then she kneeled face downward, bowing to the ground, and said to him, "Why have I found favor in your eyes that you should notice me when I am a foreigner?" Boaz answered her, "I have been made fully aware of everything that you have done for your mother-in-law since the death of your husband, and how you have left your father and mother and the land of your birth, and have come to a people that you did not know before. May the LORD repay you for your kindness, and may your reward be full from the LORD, the God of Israel, under whose wings you have come to take refuge."

Boaz noticed Ruth because of her loyalty. The way that I see this is that her loyalty drew her blessing to her. Similar to Ruth's life, I began to notice the blessings of the Lord that started coming as I drew closer to the Lord in my own life. I received favor because of my obedience. Now, I wasn't loyal to receive the blessings, neither was I loyal to the blessings, but my loyalty was to the One that my soul loved, which brought the blessing to me and my household. As I followed the Lord, I saw that as He spoke and I listened, and as He led and I followed, His plans for my life began to unfold and I was blessed more than I could even fathom, or imagine, for myself. This made me fall more in love with the Lord, not because I got what I wanted all of the time, but because even in times when I was unsure where He was leading, I knew that His plan was good. This is where my faith came in. I am encouraged by Hebrews 11:6 which says, *"But without faith, it is impossible to please Him, for he who comes to God must believe that He is and that He is a rewarder of those who diligently seek Him."*

Ruth had to follow specific instructions from the one that could redeem her. In her following those instructions, she also had to have faith. Faith is not easy when you don't know what the path may look like. Ruth did not know what the relationship would look like with Boaz, but she had to rely on her faith to follow the process that was put before her. We don't know the timing of her following Boaz's instructions, but whatever it was, she followed it. There are many times that we don't know the timing and the process of the plan that God has us on, but we can rest assured that His plans are perfect.

As women of God, God desires us to follow His plans, and love Him, knowing that we serve a good God who will reward us as we diligently seek Him, this helps us to have faith in Him. The God-seeking life brings us peace, it brings us life, and it brings us a legacy. I can attest to this as since I started following the Lord's leading in my life as a young 17-year-old, and I have seen the goodness of the Lord follow my life in return. The blessing of my husband and my children has been part of the beautiful package of legacy that the Lord had for me. As I look back throughout my life, that first real experience with the Holy Spirit set me on fire as I became loyal to Him and never looked back. I vowed that day that I would follow Him and that He would be my God. I would've never thought out of my love and loyalty for the Lord, that this life that I have been blessed with would be birthed.

"Then the women said to Naomi, "Blessed is the LORD who has not left you without a redeemer (grandson, as heir) today, and may his name become famous in Israel. May he also is to you one who restores life and sustains your old age; for your daughter-in-law, who loves you and is better to you than seven sons, has given birth to him."

RUTH

Not only did Ruth's loyalty and obedience bring blessings to her, but it also brought blessings to those who were attached to her. The one that she was loyal to heaped blessings, as well. This also testifies to the goodness of God in Ruth's life as well as mine. Because I was loyal in love with my God, the blessings of the Lord were not just given to me, but also to my husband and my children, who will continue to reap the blessings because of my obedience and love for God. May this encourage you as a reader to fall in love with the person of the Holy Spirit, make Him your Lord, follow Him all of the days of your life, and like Ruth, watch the blessing of the Lord fall upon you and the legacy that follows you.

Esther

Diahanna Wright, *53 years old*

"And Mordecai had brought up Hadassah, that is, Esther, his uncle's daughter, for she had neither father nor mother. The young woman was lovely and beautiful. When her father and mother died, Mordecai took her as his own daughter." Esther 2:7

Allow me to introduce myself, my name is Diahanna Wright, and I was an Orphan. When I look at the story of Esther, I can definitely relate, not to the natural orphan, but the spiritual aspect of one. As we read about Esther, we see the young girl whose parents were deceased, having to depend on someone who didn't physically give birth to her, but who was a family member.

Esther was a beautiful young girl whose parents died and was handled with care by Uncle Mordecai; he was very strict but patient with her due to the circumstance, he knew she was special. In reading Esther, I've always seen myself; yes, my mother has transitioned and my father is still living, but growing up as the only girl, I felt like an orphan. Orphan in the sense of not knowing my identity and always having someone saying who I was to them, what I could do for them, and never growing up embracing me as an individual.

When I was born, my name was Diahann, but as I grew older and could defend me, I wanted a name change, so my parents changed it to Diahanna. Esther, she was under the care of Mordecai who instructed her with godly wisdom because he made a promise to care for her. Growing up, I was always different and felt left out, although I was very well known. Growing up, there was a sense of feeling different from the others in my family. The feeling of *I'm the only girl like Esther with an assignment from God at an early age.*

Esther was definitely on an assignment, and as I read about her life, I wondered if she ever wanted to do certain things in her life but because of her culture, she was unable to walk in that freedom. Can you imagine yourself being inducted by soldiers to become a part of what I call *The Beautification 12 Month Beauty Treatment* amongst other ladies in the field. I am sure you haven't, and probably never will. Did Esther feel abandoned at a young age? I can say I did, because although I had my parents, I was different and because I didn't understand at such a young age, it led me to feeling like an Orphan.

What is an Orphan? In the Oxford Dictionary, an Orphan is defined as a child whose parents are dead. In the Bible, an orphan spirit attaches to a person who has experienced extreme rejection in their life. It creates separation, anxiety, and fear, and can totally end in trauma. Esther, because of her replica Mordecai, who was also family, probably didn't experience such trauma, because she had a figure that would support her, love her, and watch over her soul because he made a promise.

The promise in my life was made by my great grandmother. When she transitioned at 105 years old, she had prayed for me for years, covered me, and watched over my soul to assure that I would live and not die and declare the Works of The Lord. I was that *Esther* in my family. My grandmother, who was my Mordecai in the Spirit, was giving my parents instructions for me at an early age. Just as Esther, as I grew up, there was a smell of purity within us; God knew the plans He had for us.

ESTHER

"For I know the thoughts and plans that I have for you, says the Lord, thoughts and plans for welfare and peace and not for evil, to give you hope in your final outcome" Jeremiah 29:11, AMPC.

There was something very delicate and intriguing about the 12-month beauty treatment. Before you and I can go and present ourselves to the King, whether natural or spiritual, we must be cleansed, we must go through a treatment from all of the brokenness in our lives. Esther had to be cleansed of all the "bacteria" from being a young Jewish girl into the hands of the palace officials preparing her for the King. Although they had no idea she was of Jewish origin, she was deemed "unclean," as were the many other prospects for Queen. I, too, had to be set free from rejection, and trauma, so that a people could be free, just like Esther.

When I was a young girl, I was always told, "Diahanna, you have a people to attend to," but being a young teenager, I never understood the depth of that statement. A lot of times, we say that we want to be like others, not knowing that the Lord already gave us our own identity.

After Esther went through her treatment, she was ordained as a wife by The Lord, using the soldiers and palace officials to pick her for the King. She became a Wife, a Queen, to King Ahasuerus beforehand by her Favor with God. I can recall growing up and being chosen as the one in the family to speak, to stand up, and to defend, to go before others and be that one God would use for His glory. When I read about Queen Esther having to set up a dinner for Haman, meeting Mordecai, having meetings, and talking to the officials, I see myself.

As I matured, my parents started giving me things to do that were way over my age capacity, but it taught me how to become a leader to others, how to lead others to a place of safety and security. I would fight for others to make them feel safe and trustworthy. Growing up, I would set barriers to stop the bad people from coming into my neighborhood. As a teenager, I would stand at the corner of my neighborhood and announce and inquire of anyone that came on the street if I didn't know them, which would lead me to go to all of my neighbor's houses knocking on the doors to make sure that everyone was okay.

I was an Esther, a prototype of Jesus. So, I say this to encourage those reading this, please know your identity, you are not an Orphan but you've been adopted by Jesus Christ. You are not rejection, you do not have low self-esteem, and you are not inadequate, but you are *Special* to God and He loves you so much, from everlasting to everlasting, You are the Apple of His Eye.

"But you are a chosen race, a royal priesthood, a dedicated nation, [God's] own purchased, special people, that you may set forth the wonderful deeds and display the virtues and perfections of Him Who called you out of darkness into His marvelous light" 1 Peter 2:9, AMPC.

The *Proverbs* 31 Woman

Catherine Harmon, *49 years old*

> "Who can find a virtuous and capable wife? She is more precious than rubies." Proverbs 31:10

Who can find a virtuous wife who is far more than rubies? This is a scripture used often to guide women to teach us how to be beautiful, virtuous wives. The Book of Proverbs goes on to say how trustworthy she is and how she will do her husband well every day of her waking life. Her good deeds include working really hard in her strength to go above and beyond finding food, cooking, tending to the poor and needy, etc. Other parts of the chapter include what kind of character she possesses, such as she has no fear, she is wise, kind, efficient and diligent, while presenting herself as royalty in her fine clothing and stature. According to this chapter, she really is phenomenal. But, my question is, "Why is this even a question in the Bible to ask about a woman or better yet, are men even truly searching for this type of "virtuous wife?" When I got divorced, I stayed single for almost three years without dating anyone. During this time, I reflected on the different men I dated in my pre-marriage years, including my ex-husband. What stood out to me the most is how these relationships were established. I can't say I was in any of these relationships because I was a virtuous woman. It wasn't because I did not know how to work, tend to the needy, be diligent, or go far beyond or more, because I can say I had those values and virtues as a woman. It was because I wasn't the most important part of what the chapter describes in Proverbs 31 that stood out above all, which reads as follows:

"Charm is deceptive, and beauty does not last: but a woman who fears the Lord will be greatly praised" Proverbs 31:30.

I didn't grow up in a household where the Lord was the ruler in our home. We did not go to church on a regular basis; we did not read the Bible to understand God's character or His love for us. We may have talked about Him here and there, or visited a church on Easter Sunday or at some point, but to say He was number one in our home was not the case. If you ask my kids what they think of me today, they will probably say that Jesus is the most important part of our home. What I know today about the Lord, being a single woman in today's society, is something I believe would have shaped my entire dating experience differently with the choices of men in my life and how I am presented to them. What is important to me now when dating is a firm stature to know I am in the Lord and He is who identifies me as a virtuous woman. I am not saying any of the men I dated were bad people. They were kind men, but when I look back, I realize the most important part of being a virtuous woman is having the fear and reverence of the Lord. I did not truly have that back in my early days when dating.

Charm and beauty has been used over time for women to believe this is where our value is most important. How to obtain beauty is everywhere, from designer clothing to plastic surgery, best makeup products to image distortion. We can buy products that can laser undesirable areas of our bodies and skin. We can enhance our beauty with false products to attach where we feel needed most. I, by all means, am not judging any woman who chooses to enhance her beauty, because as women, we can appreciate a thing or two about it. Whether it is longer eyelashes, hair extensions, powdered nails, tighter skin through surgery, or breast lifts, we have options. Of course, God would want all of His daughters to be natural in our appearances because He is the One who created us. In His eyes, there is nothing wrong with His Creation. We are beautiful no matter what. What makes it wrong is when we put our trust in these things, believing it is the way of becoming a virtuous woman for a husband to find as beautiful and valuable. Based on Proverbs 31:30, what is found to make women greatly praised and valuable is the fear they have in the Lord. Our true strength and beauty comes from the Lord God above all else. When you read Proverbs 31, there is not one chapter to magnify and point out the flaws we have for not being such a wife or woman. Many of us do have these values of a Proverbs 31 woman. We can show that we are trustworthy, how to naturally comfort and encourage, we have great jobs and careers, how to have working hands to succeed in what we do. There are many women who can fit this profile of being a *virtuous woman* if we go based on that solely. But, what I wanted to make very clear about this chapter that is often overlooked is who it is written for, and why.

"The words of King Lemuel, the oracle, which his mother taught him: "What, O my son? And what, O son of my womb? And what [shall I advise you], O son of my vows" Proverbs 31:1-2, AMP.

King Lemuel is not mentioned much in Scripture, but take note that this was simply a letter of advice for him as a king from his mother. This man was put in position to be a mighty king and lead the people he was in charge of. His name means, "for God" or "devoted to God". So, we see this was a man after God's heart and that he had a desire to do things that were led by God. Being a leader under God's direction is so very important and over time, God has made it very clear what He expects of men who arc under His submission. We see the many men whom He declared as under His submission, familiar names include: Adam, Abraham, David, Solomon, and Samson. But the one thing these men had in common was being led to sin by the woman, or women, in their lives in one way or another, listening to the women's voice and not God's voice first. Eve helped Adam to sin by giving him the forbidden fruit; Sarah helped Abraham to have a child that was not the promised child by God and told him to have sexual relations with her maid; Bathsheba helped David with his lustful desires by consensually having sexual relations with him; the many wives of Solomon helped him turn his heart to other gods and not the one true Lord God; and Delilah helped Samson fall to his death. So, what was this letter to the king about? It was wisdom from his mother to stop falling for folly women and find a good wife who will help him continue to be a great leader under God's submission.

"Do not give your [generative] strength to women [neither foreign wives] in marriages of alliances, nor [concubines], Nor your ways to that which destroys kings" Proverbs 31:3, AMP.

This mother is aware of what some women are capable of when they are not in submission unto the Lord. That it is very easy for men to fall and listen to a woman's voice when they should be listening for God's voice first. How some women can help destroy his kingsmanship. This letter was to show King Lemuel that there are many woman who, because of their own weaknesses, can help him fall, but there are also women who understand how to be a virtuous wife. Being a virtuous wife in full submission to the Lord is key, as the Word says. In doing so, she is able to fulfill the fullness of her role. Read Proverbs 31:10-12, AMP. This is the kind of woman King Lemuel's mother is guiding her son to find. The two-fold question is, "was it really that hard to find a woman like that in those days and is it today? The answer is it is hard to find a woman like that these days. We live in a time where a woman can "do bad all by herself." Where beauty, vanity, and lustful images are more important than God. Where it's her body, her choice. Where women have to be more powerful than men, or equal to them. But this was never the way of our Lord. We can blame it on the lack of leadership men have in today's world and the lack of full submission to God, because, yes, they have become weaker men and are not holding themselves account-able in the Lord. But, as women, we also have to take blame in not being fully submitted to the Lord ourselves, and looking like the women of the world. So, how do you know when men are looking for a virtuous woman, or wife? Read Proverbs 31:28-30, AMP.

Since my divorce and the break I took just being in the Lord, I tried to get back into dating again. I was in a few relationships did not last very long for various reasons. I believed that I was ready because I was in the Lord more than I have ever been before. I am daily striving to be that Proverbs 31 woman. However, I question why it seems so hard to be with a man who is truly submitted unto the Lord, and are they really looking for a Proverb's 31 woman? I began to get discouraged because this seems nonexistent. There are many who appear to have a form of godliness, but deny the power of the Lord and should be turned away from according to 2 Timothy 3: 5-7. Some were really kind men. God has removed me from this place of seeking to a place of full fear and reverence of Him, so He is able to lead me. The husband in Proverbs says that there are many women who are noble and do well, but the one he found as his wife excels above them all. Why, because she fears the Lord.

This brings me to Proverbs 18:22, *"He who finds a wife, finds a good thing and obtains favor from the Lord."* Yes, there are men still seeking a virtuous woman, or wife, and as they are under submission, they will find her. She is favor he receives only by seeking the Lord. God has me in a place of preparation, serving Him. He has also restored a relationship with me to a man who is an example of a godly man, filled with the Holy Spirit, serves the Lord, and has a heart fully for Him. That man is my biological father who I was estranged from all of my life until I reached my 40's. My dad has shown me what a true man looks like submitted unto the Lord. God restored our relationship and we now do a ministry together called, *Bible Chat Central* that launched on YouTube where we discuss the Bible chapter by chapter to point people to the Lord. It is because of this man that I am learning so much from as he washes me with the Word and builds me higher in Christ as a radiant Church, like our Lord does. I believe one reason God restored our relationship is so that when He sends the right man for me, I will completely recognize him as the one God sent.

I encourage single women to be so in love with the Lord, so He can transform you into the woman set aside just for Him first, that when He is ready, He will reveal you to the man that is looking for you. For the wives, please continue to be an example of what a virtuous wife looks like in the Lord.

Abigail

Jenilee Samuel, *40 years old*

> "The name of the man was Nabal, and the name of his wife Abigail.
> And she was a woman of good understanding and beautiful appearance; but
> the man was harsh and evil in his doings. He was of the house of Caleb."
> 1 Samuel 25:3

Have you ever encountered a woman who just strikes you as stunning! (Yes, we girls notice this just as much as anyone.) She is genuinely beautiful and lovely, takes good care of herself, probably smells good, and has this warm quality that sets people at ease because she is so kind. It makes you begin to wonder, "Who is she and how can we be friends?" Women like this always feel like such a precious discovery and great bestie potential! It's like there's a little part of my soul that is intrigued to know her, so I can be *like* her. Meeting a woman like this speaks to the depths of our female essence and makes us aspire to be this way, as well. Well, apparently there are a few women like this in Scripture, and Abigail is one of them. *"Abigail was intelligent and beautiful"* (1 Samuel 25:3, NIV). As I continued to explore her journey, the thing I related to was that she had someone close to her (her husband in this case) who was harsh, mean, and a wicked man. We all probably know someone in our lives who is like this. Maybe a teacher, a parent, a spouse, a sibling, a school bully, or a boss. But there's something particularly harmful when you have to live under the same roof as that person, as did Abigail. Often, when you're in a close relationship with someone who is toxic and mean, disrespectful and unloving, manipulative or controlling, it affects your mental health and your perspective of yourself if you don't have a healthy way to process that treatment. It can make YOU cold and hard, insecure, unsure of yourself, paralyzed into non-action, critical and nasty, or any other variety of coping qualities.

When we maintain relationships with people who are quick to anger, we can pick up some of their habits, and develop coping habits that aren't healthy, endangering our soul (Proverbs 22:24-25). This means "to become capable of great sin". When you're constantly exposed to someone of anger, it becomes destructive to you, causing you to act out sinful behavior that isn't like you. You begin to take on a survival mindset, where virtue, wisdom, and even daily tasks become harder to exhibit because your soul's energy is more focused on simply surviving the mistreatment. Abigail, however, doesn't appear to have been impacted in this manner. She evidently found healthy ways to deal with him to protect her heart, possibly keeping her distance, managing to maintain a beautiful soul.

In 1 Samuel 25, David was not yet king and in fact, he was running from King Saul who was hell-bent on killing him due to his awful jealousy. David went down to the wilderness of Maon to stay off Saul's radar, where there was a wealthy man named Nabal (Abigail's husband) who owned property near Carmel, sheep and goats, and it was shearing season. While Abigail was sensible and lovely, Nabal was *"crude and mean in all his dealings"* (vs 3). They must have had an arranged marriage! When David heard that Nabal was shearing his sheep, he sent ten men with a message of peace and a request for Nabal's kindness to share food and provision for them as they traveled. It stated that when Nabal's shepherds stayed among David's men, none were harmed or stolen from. They were treated with kindness, and now David was hoping for a returned favor. Instead, Nabal got nasty and sneered at the young servants (vs 10-11). So, David's men returned and reported what Nabal said. *"Get your swords!"* David's replied. He charged off with 400 of his men to kill Nabal and his entire household. Meanwhile, one of Nabal's servants heard what happened and how he responded to David's request, and hurried off to tell Abigail (vs. 14-17, NLT). Abigail comes on the scene to make history receiving the endorsement of being "Intelligent and Beautiful".

Beauty Code 1: A beautiful and intelligent woman creates safety for those around her and exudes confidence.

Firstly, the servants knew they could go to her and be heard. She was a safe person to them. Secondly, in verse 18 it says, *"Abigail wasted no time."* She quickly gathered a lot of good food, wine, and desserts and packed them on donkeys, saying to her servants *"Go on ahead. I will follow you shortly."* Abigail wasted no time. This struck me first because when I had walked through a season with a very toxic person for sixteen years, the impact of their toxicity on me caused me to question and second guess myself *constantly*. This was an indicator of how much the abuse had impacted me because my natural temperament is to be decisive and confident, but the toxic behavior had gutted me of that. However, one of the early signs of Abigail's strength of heart was that she acted *quickly* and with *confidence*. She didn't have time to second guess herself or people would die. She embraced confidence in her decision making to smooth out this conflict her foolish husband had created.

Beauty Code 2: True beauty operates with discretion and boundaries.

Abigail demonstrated discretion in a few ways. Discretion is defined as the quality of having good judgement and discernment. Aside from the obvious discretion she demonstrated by making sure to fulfill David's original request for food (in abundance), she had discretion in what she *didn't* share with her husband. In most cases, it's important that we share our plans with our husbands, so they can be on board and in agreement with us. But in this instance, Abigail recognized that Nabal was not deserving of the knowledge of her plan. Proverbs says, *"He who is given a trust, must prove trustworthy."* Based on his past actions and how he had created this mess in the first place, Nabal was not trustworthy enough to know of her plan. So, she did not tell her husband at the risk of him getting involved and making the situation worse. **This was discretion**. Now, don't hear me wrong and think I'm endorsing hiding things from your husband. What I'm saying is, *people who are given certain privileges must prove responsible, no matter who you are*. This is a principle of healthy boundaries which is at the heart of being able to make discretionary decisions and to be a healthy and intelligent person. Even with your spouse. In this case, Abigail did end up telling Nabal what happened, but it wasn't until later, when he was sober, and it was a good moment for it.

Beauty Code 3: Humility and taking responsibility are the currency of true leadership. They are both beautiful and wise, and position you to make a difference!

Abigail demonstrated humility and taking responsibility (vs. 23-24, NLT). She came with no presumption, very aware that he was angry and had a right to be. He had been mistreated by her husband, and she knew very well that if she was going to have any success here, humility was essential. However, she stepped into leadership the moment she took responsibility. When someone takes responsibility for a situation, they regain the power to shift and change things which is a position of leadership. *Not a title, but influence.* True leadership is simply the ability to influence change, and her beauty was in her servant leadership.

Beauty Code 4: Do not make excuses for wrongdoing. It is both beautiful and intelligent to acknowledge the truth, we simply must do it in love.

Personally, I love that she did not make excuses for Nabal (vs. 25). In fact, some would say she threw him under the bus, but the reality is she didn't. She just acknowledged the facts, which brought empathy into the situation for David's sake, and also kept her from having to carry the unfair weight of Nabal's foolishness. She acknowledged the facts: he was wrong and David's experience with him was not David's fault. This is not dishonoring, this is walking in truth. When we seek to protect others by making excuses for their behavior, we are no longer walking in truth. God never calls sin by pet names. He addresses it for what it is, kindly, but he doesn't make excuses, nor should we.

Beauty Code 5: Use your words to diffuse conflict by calling people into their higher self and reminding them who they are.

From verses 26-31, Abigail proceeds to remind him who he is. This is a very powerful discourse she goes into as she *calls him into his higher self.* This also pulls him out of his triggered "fight or flight" mode, and allows his brain to remember who he is. Embedded in her words is a sense of honor and respect for his character and the *good*

David she knows him to be. She even contrasts him against Nabal by blessing him with a blessing that those who would try to harm him would be cursed like Nabal. When dealing with people, it is important, especially in conflict, that we can call people back into their higher self. This was incredible wisdom.

Beauty Code 6: A beautiful and wise woman believes in the greatness in people, making them feel seen.

Woah! Okay. If he wasn't in love with her before, he is now (vs. 30). Remember, David is being chased by Saul who is actually King at the time. He is on the run. Being hunted. Feeling like anything but a king. However, he is holding onto the promises of God not yet delivered. She spoke into a very vulnerable place. She reminds him of God's promises, stoking his faith and calling him back to his one true mission. She is simultaneously showing that she believes in him and believes in the call of God on his life. And she is also looking out for his future reputation, while speaking to his current one. She is reminding him that he is a hero. No wonder he ends up asking her to be his wife! Oh wait... no spoilers. You'll have to read the full passage! If Abigail had not responded as she did, many lives would have ended, including hers. If she had not been killed, she would have been widowed and lost to poverty after losing her husband and all their men. But because she acted quickly, (which David also acknowledged), and because she responded with so much wisdom and beauty, the Lord preserved David from tarnishing his name with innocent bloodshed and from her own demise as a widow, or possibly death.

At the bottom of beauty and intelligence is the spirit of a queen. A woman who is not made smaller by difficult circumstances or people. A woman who is courageous and confident, who embraces servant leadership and the shrewdness of boundaries, discretion, being a safe person for others, and calling to the greatness in those around them. Being beautiful and intelligent is learnable and doable. You, too, can be the "Abigail" in the lives of the people around you, and I have no doubt we will see God promote and use you in ways that you couldn't have imagined, otherwise.

Rahab

Beverly Wardlow, *73 years young*

"Now Joshua the son of Nun sent out two men from Acacia Grove to spy
secretly, saying, "Go, view the land, especially Jericho." So they went,
and came to the house of a harlot named Rahab, and lodged there."
Joshua 2:1

Today... you will meet the "you" that you always knew you were.
Rahab—pagan prostitute; Idol worshipper. It was finally happening, it was finally here... destiny was at her door... and was
knocking loudly. She had wanted change, had even prayed to her
idol gods for change, but nothing had ever happened. Her gods
had never answered her or delivered her from anything. She was so tired
of being used by men who only wanted her for her body and her beauty.
She had prayed and hoped for someone to see her as more than just a
body for hire.

Rahab woke up every morning with the same thought... Is this all
that I'm supposed to be? Is this all that it's going to be for me? But when
two strangers came to her house for hiding, instinctively she knew that
they were different from every other man who had knocked on her door.
She gasped at the realization that these men were Israelites. These men
were enemies of Jericho. Everyone in the city was talking about the huge
army of Israelites who had set up camp outside of Jericho, pitching tents

across the Jordan river a few days prior. These men were enemies of Jericho. She also realized that these two men knew the unknown, unnamed God that had been talked about, and everyone was afraid of, and Rahab wanted to know more. She had heard about their God *Yahweh*, that He was the God of the Israelites; she has heard stories about him raining down fire from heaven–somehow, she just felt that their god was the true God. Their God wasn't carved out of stone or clay, their God was real; in fact, she was told that their old leader, Moses, had seen him in person. If this God could make a dry path through the Red Sea for His people to get away from danger, then maybe this was the change that she was hoping for. If this was the God that destroyed the Amorite army, then maybe, just maybe, He could be her God.

But before she could find out who their God was to them, she received word that the soldiers were coming through and were checking nearby houses for the two spies that were spotted in the vicinity. Although she did not know these strangers, neither did they know her, it shocked her that she wasn't afraid of them. There was an instant connection, and she immediately decided that she would aid them by hiding them on her roof under flax branches from Jericho's soldiers.

You never know how strong you are until being
strong is your only choice.

Her heart jumped at the sound of the soldiers banging on her door and before she could even get to the door, they burst into her home demanding to know where the spies were and strangely, somehow, she was able to remain calm, although her heart was continuing to race, and she asked them who they were talking about. Lying was something that came with her profession, and she was good at it. So, she told them that the spies had left the city and if they hurried, they might be able to catch them and capture them. As soon as the soldiers left, she made her way up to the roof to speak to the spies.

Rahab took great risks to save the Israelite spies that had the potential of destroying her life and that of her family. She told them that everyone in Jericho was aware of the Israelite camps on the other side of the Jordan River, and everyone was afraid of the army that have their God in their encampment. She shared that the men of her city were frightened, and their hearts were melted, that there was no strength nor courage left in the Jericho men's hearts. Then, she made the biggest decision of her life to align herself with the Israelite spies.

The Contract: Joshua 2: 12-21,

"Now then, please swear to me by the LORD that you will show kindness to my family, because I have shown kindness to you. Give me a sure sign that you will spare the lives of my father and mother, my brothers, and sisters, and all who belong to them—and that you will save us from death. Our lives for your lives!" the men assured her. "If you don't tell what we are doing, we will treat you kindly and faithfully when the LORD gives us the land." So she let them down by a rope through the window, for the house she lived in was part of the city wall. She said to them, "Go to the hills so the pursuers will not find you. Hide yourselves there three days until they return, and then go on your way." Now the men had said to her, "This oath you made us swear will not be binding on us unless, when we enter the land, you have tied this scarlet cord in the window through which you let us down, and unless you have brought your father and mother, your brothers and all your family into your house. If any of them go outside your house into the street, their blood will be on their own heads; we will not be responsible. As for those who are in the house with you, their blood will be on our head if a hand is laid on them. But if you tell what we are doing, we will be released from the oath you made us swear." "Agreed," she replied. "Let it be as you say." So, she sent them away, and they departed. And she tied the scarlet cord in the window."

Isn't it powerful that the Israelites put the blood on their doorposts to be saved from the angel of death, and that the spies gave her a representation of the color red, which represents the blood... yes Jesus Christ is clearly represented in the Old Testament. Rahab's life is the perfect illustration that our sin doesn't define us in God's eyes. God's grace is so big that no one can say that their sin is too big for His grace to cover. He covers our sins with such grace. He started the relationship with us FIRST! 1 John 4:19 explains it so clearly: *We love Him because He first loved us.*

God sometimes confounds us by using the most unsavory individuals (in our eyes). He's used murderers, thieves, prostitutes, adulterers, liars and yes, even cowards to fulfill His purpose, by transforming their lives so miraculously that it leaves no doubt to the soul-saving, life transforming grace giving God that He is. That is something only the triune God could do. God used Rahab the prostitute to illustrate His redemptive power in this poignant story.

Question? What message is God using in your life to tell His redemptive story?

"For the message of the cross is foolishness to those who are perishing, but to us who are being saved it is the power of God. For it is written: "I will destroy the wisdom of the wise; the intelligence of the intelligent I will frustrate... **For the foolishness of God is wiser than human wisdom, and the weakness of God is stronger than human strength. Brothers and sisters, think of what you were when you were called. God chose the lowly things of this world and the despised things—and the things that are not—to nullify the things that are, so that no one may boast before him..."** 1 Corinthians 1:18-31 (Read in its entirety.)

Isn't it amazing that God uses the very thing that wounded you or made you fall to re-write your story? Maybe your life's story wasn't as dramatic as Rahab's, but we were all born into sin, and at some point, of our failings, God redeemed us by the blood of Jesus. He cleansed us from our failures and sin, threw our sins away, and saw us as new creatures—WOW!

Rahab's moment of salvation came <u>at the very moment</u> she started speaking about God as a reality–she declared in this scripture, that the <u>Lord God IS GOD in heaven above and on the earth below</u>. Salvation happened and declared!

"When we heard of it, our hearts melted in fear and everyone's courage failed because of you, **for the LORD your God is God in heaven above and on the earth below"** Joshua 2:11b.

Her entire life was changed at that moment.

RAHAB

"But without faith it is impossible to please Him, for he who comes to God must believe that He is, and that He is a rewarder of those who diligently seek Him" Hebrews 11:6.

Looking at the lineage of Jesus Christ, it has a prostitute (Rahab), that is a testament of God's grace. There is a murderer and an adulterer (King David), that is a testament of God's endless mercy and forgiveness. This is such a powerful testament that who we were before He cleansed us is of no consequence to God. Once He cleanses us and washes the sin out of our hearts, we are truly a new creation in Him. He no longer sees the previously sinful nature that we were; He only sees us as blood washed saints. This powerful story goes on to see not only Rahab and her family saved. The direction from Joshua for the priests and soldiers (mighty men of valor and men of war) was to walk once, each day around the walls of Jericho for 6 days, in total silence as per the direction of the Lord, but on the 7th day, to walk with the seven priests, who were instructed to blow their trumpets around the walls 7 times. They were instructed that when they heard the long blast made with the ram's horn and the shout of the trumpets, the soldiers were to shout with a GREAT shout.

This powerful demonstration of doing exactly what God instructed them to do, resulted in the powerful walls of Jericho to fall at their feet, destroying all vestiges of protection that the city had moments before. The walls of Jericho fell, but Rahab's house that was built into the walls of the city remained stable. The Israelites took the city, as God promised that it was theirs. Everything, every man, woman, child, and cattle was destroyed, because of the idolatry and sin in the city. But because Rahab kept her contract with the Israelite spies, Joshua commanded his soldiers to spare Rahab and her family.

Rahab's contract with the Israelites cemented her name, not only in this book but later as a direct descendant of Jesus Christ. What a powerful reward for protecting God's chosen people.

The Samaritan Woman

April Albrecht, *69 years old*

"Then the woman of Samaria said to Him, "How is it that You, being a Jew, ask a drink from me, a Samaritan woman?" For Jews have no dealings with Samaritans." John 4:9

O
h, what a day this was for the Samaritan woman at the well. Little did she know of her encounter with Jesus! Soon, she would be in His presence. It's the middle of the day, and Jesus decided to stop by the well where He would encounter a Samaritan woman fetching water. Although this was the hottest time of the day, as it would turn out, they were both there for more than simply a drink of water.

"Then a woman from Samaria came to draw water. Jesus said to her, "Give Me a drink" John 4:7.

The conversation quickly changed from Jesus' physical needs to the woman's spiritual needs. As is often the case when encountering Jesus, she did not understand the significance of what He was asking. In fact, she would soon see that Jesus was talking about something completely different than what she had in mind. Fast forward some 2,000 years… my day started at 3:00am in the morning. I had been an election trainer, training people who had volunteered to work the polls on election day.

The big day was here and I found myself drinking several cups of coffee to become more alert as I am not as they say, "a morning person".

It was around the middle of the day when I pulled over to see what voting precinct I needed to go to next. I had just replaced some equipment at one location and was ready to be of service at the next stop. To my surprise, a beautiful bluebird came flying by my van with the most brilliant colors. I took my phone out of my purse to get a quick picture.

This same beautiful bird came back again except this time, it landed on my side mirror. I was very stunned at first, when does a bird land on your mirror? I was able to take a few more pictures before he flew away. As I was ready to leave that location and head off to my next precinct, that bluebird came back again. This time, he landed right on my passenger window. Wow! It was as if he was looking right at me. He had the most magnificent colors. You may already know this, but the male birds have a lot more colors on them then the females do. Does not work so much that way in the human race. Well, after he left, I had to get back to work.

I was so excited that I got those pictures but even more so that the bluebird landed on my car. I have never had that happen before. About five hours had passed, and since it was the end of the day, I needed to discard all those coffee cups that were cluttering my van. I found a strip mall with a trash can that would do the job. With cups in hand, I walked over to the receptacle. I have to say I was a little shocked at first. Laying right on top was a box, an empty box. I picked it up and noticed that the very same bird that I had taken pictures of earlier, colors and all and even the same profile of the bluebird, was on every side of that box! Wow! The box was in perfect condition with no dirt or scratches. I was stunned as I was holding it in my hands. My first thought was what a coincidence.

Everything changed when I saw the lid of the box. It *read "be still and know that I am God"* Psalm 46:10.

What!!! Be still, and know that I am God! It was as if God was speaking directly to me using the bluebird to teach me a lesson about faith.

Whether I feel His presence or not, He is always with me. Regardless of what I have done or what has been done to me, He is always with me. All I have to do is *be still and know*, in the depth of my heart, that He is God. He is all powerful and ever present. So many times, when my life was in turmoil, I would look to the sky and wish I were a bird, so I could just fly and settle onto a tree branch overlooking a lake. More than anything, I wanted peace and because of Jesus, I could have that peace. I thought about Jesus's words to His followers:

"Look at the birds. They don't plant or harvest or store food in barns, for your heavenly Father feeds them. And aren't you far more valuable to him than they are?" Matthew 6:26.

My encounter with the bluebird made this verse so real to me. If He cares for the birds in the sky, He will care for me. I am more valuable to Him than all the birds of the sky, and do you know what? So are you! You, too, can know the peace of God through a relationship with Jesus. Maybe you are carrying guilt or shame from your past, as I did from mine and are dealing with situations that you are feeling so overwhelmed with. And just when you think you can settle on a branch and be at rest for a while, you find yourself unable to sit still, like the birds in my backyard that sometimes fly from branch to branch. You find yourself stirred up by emotional pain, unable to have real peace.

God wants you to have that peace, to be able to be still and know that He is God. Through His Son, Jesus you can have that peace, the kind of peace that comes from knowing you are forgiven, that you will spend eternity in Heaven, and that Jesus will be with you every day of your life here. It doesn't matter what you have done, you can have the kind of peace that surpasses our human understanding when you have a relationship with Jesus. If He did it for me, He will do it for you. All you have to do is ask Him.

Ask Jesus to forgive you for all the wrong things you have done. He is faithful to forgive you because that is His gift to you. He promises He will never leave you or forsake you. Ask Him to be your Savior. God wants everyone to be a part of His family. To be a part of His flock, and the only way to do that is by accepting the free gift of forgiveness we get from Jesus.

God has used birds in my life to reveal His love, forgiveness, and faithfulness to me. I hope when you look up at the sky and see the birds it reminds you of how much God loves you. I may not have been at a well in the heat of the day like the Samaritan woman was where Jesus interacted with her. In my case, around the same time of day, Jesus used a beautiful little bluebird to get my attention of His presence to me.

Years before, my life was filled with guilt and shame from a life that I had been living. Let's just say I wasn't interested in wild birds or pet birds, and the only birds I was interested in were "the birds and the bees" until one day I found out I was pregnant with my precious daughter.

One of my favorite verses is Romans 8:28, which states: *"... and we know that in all things God works for the good of those who love him, who have been called according to his purpose."* I now get to see my beautiful granddaughter going off to college to be a youth pastor, which is a deep desire of her heart to reach out to those young ones trying to survive in a world that is ever changing.

"... then, leaving her water jar, the woman went back to the town and said to the people, "come, see a man who told me everything I ever did. Could this be the Messiah? They came out of their town and made their way toward him" John 4:28-30.

I believe that the Samaritan woman's first plan for the day was to fill that water jar, and then everything changed. She went and told the people about Jesus the Messiah and brought them to Him, so they could see and hear for themselves.

My first plan for the day was to go from precinct to precinct to be of service where needed. Everything changed for me when Jesus used a beautiful bluebird to remind me to *be still and know that He is God*. I want to go out and tell the world about His love, restoration, grace, and forgiveness which brings us eternal life by making a decision to follow Him. While writing this, it occurred to me that just like the Samaritan woman, God had visited me in a most unusual way, a life changing way and I want to tell everyone about it. God often uses these situations to show us what He wants us to do. Just like the Samaritan woman, in my case, it was a gift of evangelism.

"For this is what the Lord has commanded us:" 'I have made you a light for the Gentiles, that you may bring salvation to the ends of the earth."

Bluebird poem by my son Michael:

Everything changed in a moment, what a day.

A bluebird came along, headed my way. It flew right to me with magnificent display. Excitement flew not astray but with direction. As the paths perhaps it knew would soon make a strong connection. Emotion lifted high and soon to my surprise in the trash can I found a box with a bluebird on every side. As I picked up the box, no dirt, or scratches it read "be still and know that I am God," no such coincidence but brought peace that surpasses. Understanding for many to see God speaks through ordinary things.

Everything changed in a moment.

What a day. A bluebird came along head my way. His presence always there though many times we neglect it. Look up to your Creator and ask for His direction. When life is overwhelming, and that shame calls your name. Remember God's love. He will bring you through the pain. A bluebird may pass or settle on a branch. Keep your eyes open always, even throwing out the trash.

Everything changed in a moment, what a day. A bluebird came along, headed my way.

Devotional 9

Talitha Cumi

Deborah Herbert, *64 years old*

"Then He took the child by the hand, and said to her, "Talitha, cumi," which is translated, "Little girl, I say to you, arise." Mark 5:41

W hile going through the choices of the Women of the Bible to write about, I kept coming back to *Talitha Cumi*. At first, this made no sense. Because her story and my story are nothing alike. Or so I thought. In Mark 5, we read Jesus raised her from the dead, *"Gripping her firmly by the hand, He said to her, Talitha Cumi— which translated is, Little girl, I say to you arise [from the sleep of death]"* (Mark 5:41). I have six children in Heaven and three wonderful living, breathing, healthy, and happy children here on Earth, along with four grandchildren. Here is why I did not think my story was the same as Talitha Cumi. Because my story is one of many losses. Talitha Cumi means *little girl arise*. Yalad Cumi means *infant arise*. Many times over a seventeen year span, He had the opportunity to say "arise" to one of my babies. Let me briefly tell you their story.

Joshua Caleb—I was young and prayed for the tubal pregnancy to miraculously move to the correct place and live. For whatever reason, the doctor did not choose to perform immediate surgery so in my innocent, very young brain, that meant life was still possible. But no "Yalad Cumi". No "infant arise". Years later, the Lord told me my first son's name is *Joshua Caleb*. *Olivia Grace* is my little Canadian born girl. At thirteen weeks pregnant, I began cramping and to the hospital we went. I appreciated the policy in Canada. They did not immediately do a DNC. They waited for three negative tests in a row, so I had two more days to believe for the life of the baby I was carrying. Oh my goodness, I was still so young and young in faith. Although raised in a Christian home, I did not know of anyone who had asked God for such a miracle as this. But I was reading my Bible in the hospital and ministering to the nurses all the stories of the miracles of Jesus. But on the third day, no "Talitha cumi,"

Dustin was born a few years later. I didn't even know to ask for healing for him. Finally carrying a baby to term I thought all was well. He was diagnosed quickly after birth with a rare disease called Potters Syndrome and went to join both his brother and his sister in Heaven two hours after birth. I didn't understand. This is when I finally started asking God, "Why?" *Jonathan* was a different story. Diagnosed at sixteen weeks with Potters; this time, I felt older and wiser and full of faith. Sometimes, only a mustard seed of faith. And some days, *"Lord I believe, [constantly] help my weakness of faith"* (Mark 9:24). Now attending a Full Gospel Church, I thought it was the natural thing to believe for healing. Saturating myself with scriptures and books on faith. Friends, Virginia and Cherry, came every week for us to pray and believe and teach me how to soak in His Presence. I began journaling the journey in order to write a book. At the end, would be pictures of Jonathan. The *Nothing is Impossible with God* baby. I couldn't wait to share.

At twenty weeks, Jonathan no longer had a heartbeat. The Bible does say in Matthew 10:8, *"Cure the sick, raise the dead, cleanse the lepers, cast out demons."* Raise the dead. I had not gone into labor. So, we believed for the impossible. Not everyone rallied in belief for resurrection. But oh how great a relationship was formed by those who joined us in this journey; lasting friendships to this day. Jesus told Jairus, the father of the little girl in our story, *"Do not be seized with alarm and struck with fear; simply believe [in Me as able to do this] and she shall be made well"* (Luke 8:50). Mark 5:36 says: *"Only keep on believing."* So, we chose to simply believe. Though that learning season was not simple. No *Yalad Cumi*. My infant son was not raised. Jonathan was stillborn at twenty-seven weeks.

TALITHA CUMI

Joseph Alexander gave us our next opportunity to "simply believe." We found out at twenty weeks that he, too, had Potters Syndrome. We began to gather at my friend Martha's home to soak and pray before each of my doctor appointments. This was the sixth loss. I could not have continued without that time of pressing into His Presence. We desperately needed Him to be our very present help in this time of trouble (Psalm 46:1). Joseph was born at thirty-two weeks. We were able to bring him home. He lived for twenty-six hours. When he stopped breathing, we immediately went into "Yalad Cumi" mode. At 3am, friends bombarded my home to believe for resurrection. Great faith. Mustard seeds of faith. Lord, give me faith. The night before Joseph's funeral, MANY gathered at the funeral home. My parents, family members, friends, and church members. Many said to Joseph "arise" but ultimately, he joined his brothers and sisters in Heaven. Again, no *Yalad Cumi*.

So, how is my story and Talitha Cumi alike? None of my children were raised from the dead. No, my children were not healed nor raised from the dead, but there came a day when I was. Not dead physically, but oh so dead. Death that was so slow I didn't even realize it had happened. I still loved the Lord. Still worshipped. I didn't realize I was "dead." That is something we need to watch for; pay attention to. Especially if raised in church. You know what to do. You know how to pray and what to say. I knew how to be a Christian. And I was good at it. Staying busy doing Christian work. Doing all the wonderful things. And those things brought joy. But still within me was death. This prickling in my brain, always there. I noticed when I quoted scriptures, they hit this place in me. I kept dismissing it as, "Girl, you don't need to allow doubt in. You know His Word is Truth. Simply believe." Well, my head and my heart were in continuous arguments. However, I wouldn't stop and allow the argument to play out. I kept dismissing it as lack of faith and my mentality was *just keep going and everything will sort its way out along the way*. I was counting on this hurt and this pain to be something He could eventually use for good. (Genesis 50:20, AMP). I remember the day I was lying on the couch recuperating from Joseph's birth. I heard Holy Spirit say, "What are you going to do?" I knew what He was asking. I stood on the Word with all I knew how to. If the Word doesn't "work," then I'm lost. It's my foundation and at that moment, I felt my foundation had crumbled into a million pieces under my feet. I didn't know how to put those pieces back together again. I was utterly lost. Utterly dismayed.

I laid there for hours not answering. I was mad. I was hurt. I was lost. I rolled scripture after scripture and event after event through my brain. I finally replied to Him, "Where else would I go? Who else has words of life." (John 6:68, AMP). I stepped towards healing. I had to choose "life". We had three children to raise. *Faith Elizabeth*, miracle #1 was born after Dustin. *Amanda Joy*, miracle #2 was born after *Sarah Hope*; who was an early miscarriage. *James Michael* miracle #3 was born after *Jonathan*. I have come across many who did not make that same decision; to keep following Christ. They were too wounded. Dismayed. Angry as heck. I understand you. I don't condemn you. I've been you and I want to encourage you.

One day, I was cleaning up toys and I heard in my spirit, *"He who goes about sowing in tears, will one day reap a joyful harvest"* Psalm 126:5. Even though I was weeping (and weeping and weeping) holding on to what I can only describe as wounded faith, God honored that wounded, mustard seed of faith. Because that is Who He is. I didn't understand why our faith "didn't work," but I did know He is God and He is good. I learned to hold onto what Truth I could. That was all I could give Him. Life moved on. Wife, mom, and staying busy being a Christian. One night in Bible School in a class perfectly called "Faith," Holy Spirit asked me if I trusted Him and I said, "Yes." He asked me to give Him my journals, meaning all the writings and reasonings I had mulled over and over for years trying to make the Word and my experience line up. 1+1 just was not equaling 2. He asked me to hand Him my testimony, He would take care of it and to just hold onto the Bible as Truth. I felt like a ton of weight was removed. I no longer felt the need to explain my testimony. At that moment, I could go back to "simply believe." Scriptures still seemed to mock me at times but healing was taking place. So, when did my resurrection happen?

Chip Brim, a guest speaker at our church, read, *"Arise [from the depression and prostration in which circumstances have kept you—rise to a new life]! Shine (be radiant with the glory of the Lord), for your light has come and the glory of the Lord has risen upon you"* (Isaiah 60:1, AMP). I locked onto that scripture. Something in me was set free. He taught, "Arise" meant first things first. Get yourself to a higher level.

I wish I was like Talitha when I heard that; just sat up in my spirit, was hungry, ate some lunch, and lived happily every day since. But this is when my heart started to change. It was a huge step towards healing. I was starting to arise; to live again.

There were two rough marriages intermingled with all those losses of babies. This meant a lot of wounded and broken pieces needed to be put back together. A lot of Truth needed to be poured into me as I handed Him one area of hurt after the other. But listen to me well, and hear my heart please; It is worth it! Hand Him your brokenness! I cannot explain to you the richness of my relationship with the Lord. It is the sweetest! So, where does this leave us? He didn't say to six of my children, "Yalad Cumi" *infant arise*. They are all a part of our heavenly greeting committee we will see one day. Even though He didn't say to me, "Talitha Cumi," *little girl arise*. He did resurrect me, over time, through His Word. Slowly arising from the depression circumstances had left me, I was arising to a new life. Because His Word is LIFE. But I had to choose. Choose to be alive in my soul. Choose joy. Choose leaning and learning. Choose to let go of how I thought the story was supposed to go. That was a hard one. Choose to stop reasoning. Choose to no longer be angry. Choose to trust Him again. Choose to trust? He is such a GOOD GOD and He knows the thoughts and struggles we have between our brains and our hearts.

Wounded faith is the only way I know to describe it, and He has healed it through and through! One day, I saw a picture of a lady with the word "Redeemed" tattooed on her wrist, "That's it!" That is how I feel. I have been redeemed. Sackcloth pulled off. All the wrappings of thoughts and reasonings removed. Raised! I can share my testimony with joy. His Presence and my relationship with Him is unique. It was forged in fire. Forged from all the days He carried me. Permeating me with His compassion. Such appreciation of how He brought me from deep hurt when He did not utter the words I wanted Him to say over child after child. And a knowing that all my tears, while standing in what faith I knew to stand in, were like priceless seeds to Him and there would be a harvest. My prayer my sweet friend; if you can identify with even a portion of my story—if you did not hear the words: "Talitha Cumi" for a loved one, realize YOU are the one who now needs to be raised. I say in absolute love, by the power of Holy Spirit, "Arise, Arise, Arise!!!"

Mary Magdalene

Bronwen Healy, *48 years old*

"Now when He rose early on the first day of the week, He appeared first to Mary Magdalene, out of whom He had cast seven demons." Mark 16:9

My past is not my future. Every time I get asked, "How can you share your story with no shame attached to it," I think of one woman and the way she chose to lay down her life to live in the fullness of the resurrection life that Jesus died on the Cross at Calvary for her to have. I think about all the other women like her and me, that might be on the other side of sharing my story and I remember the broken, angry, lonely, hard-hearted younger me that met Him in the midst of the deepest and darkest time of my life. I cannot help but reply, "How could I not? He forgave me for it all, loved me back to life, and gave me hope for the future. I am loved and I want every person whose path I cross to know that He is kind and sets people like us truly free, so that we can live free, indeed!" When I get to Heaven, I will be embracing my beloved Mother and then looking for Mary Magdalene to embrace and thank her for her story. She gave me hope then; she gives me hope now. Because of her, and all those like us, I tell my story. Jesus spoke to her by the empty tomb; she was weeping and blinded by her own grief and loss, and saw Him, but did not fully see Him. He then spoke her new name and she knew it was Him. Read John 20:16-18, HCSB. We all have a story to tell; no matter who we are, what we have done, or what has been done to us. Mary Magdalene, me, you; we each hold a story within us, a story to be told. Revelation 12:11

reminds us of the power of sharing our stories with one another; to remember the goodness of God, the power of redemption, and that there are other people's freedom and healing on the other side of us partnering with Him and His resurrection power.

Every redemption story starts somewhere, right? Just like Mary Magdalene, the love and comfort of Jesus came into my life during the darkest chapter. He gave me a new heart and forgave me of my past, gave me a brand-new life and hope for my future; and just like her, my past is not my future. That said, my past helped to shape, make, and break me and found me in a place where I needed His redeeming love and to fully grasp my wild and steadfast love for Him. Now, we must go back in time to fully understand. I was born in Melbourne, Australia in 1975, to a family that knew pain through the destructive nature of the aggressive alcoholism that kept my dad bound for many years. Our entire family was consumed by the disease. I did not know any different, even as a little 2-year-old, to grab the last of the beer can and drink it; and we have the 70's-style photos to prove it. My Mom's mom lived with us for my first three years, and she, too, was controlled by alcohol and eventually died at a young age; destroyed by the fuel that kept her from living the full life she so desperately wanted to live. My parents did not know how to process the grief and loss, and just like Mary Magdalene at the tomb; they were blinded by it, all the while trying to shield me and my older brother from the aftermath of the void that was created when she was gone. My Dad's drinking worsened and just before my third birthday, he sought help to get sober through a 12-step program. The fellowship he and my mom found was both healing and transformative for them, as they now knew they were not alone on their journeys. They continued to love us the best way they knew how. The phone was always ringing, and the kettle was always on the boil as my mom welcomed all who needed a friend and a listening ear; she had found her true calling in coming alongside others and being a mutual support for them. Our lives changed because of the choices they made to pursue connection and healing through community.

My Mom collected the well-known Serenity Prayer, and it was seen on every possible wall and corner in our home. We had no idea how pivotal that prayer would become in the years to follow, and the ways my mom would cling to it for hope, but God knew, and in His knowing,

He engraved it on her heart, and mine. When I was thirteen years old, we moved to another state to live in Brisbane; leaving behind my then 18-year-old brother and every friend and community I had ever known. I attended an elite private girls' school and quickly started to realise that I did not fit in. I did not know who I was, I did not have any foundations of identity to lean into and nobody to cling to; I was lost, and I felt so alone. Those feelings forced me to try to find ways to fit in but ultimately, led to me wanting to withdraw and trying to escape the feelings altogether. Such a dangerous combination, a family with a history of addiction, loneliness, and wanting to be numb. I started to smoke cigarettes at age fourteen, in an attempt to be cool. Then, I hosted a birthday party for my 14th birthday and the attendees consumed so much alcohol that my mom had to call the police to contain their behaviours. I was searching, wanting to fit in; with no clue of who I truly was. Lost and confused.

The journey of exploration continued for many years and came to a huge turning point when I moved schools for my Senior years, to focus on film and television; believing that someday, I would end up making movies in Hollywood. I soon discovered that most of the students at the new school smoked marijuana every day and took other chemical drugs on the weekends. Again, I did not fit in, believing that this time it was for the right reasons. These wild and wonderful humans embraced me for me, even though I still did not know who I truly was, and they encouraged me to push my own limits with my creativity, and I did. Once I knew I had the grades to get into the University degree I wanted to pursue, I pushed my own limits in new and unhealthy ways when I started to explore the world of drugs. It started with marijuana and quickly turned to speed, LSD, ecstasy, cocaine, and any other 'party drug' I could get my hands on. My weekends quickly became longer than the days of the week, my brain more scattered, and my identity even blurrier than ever before. I was lost and confused, and now I was using drugs every day to mask my own reality from myself.

I was sleeping around and in and out of dysfunctional relationships, trying to find out who I really was. I was literally looking for love in all the wrong places, with no clue there was One who could fully see me and longing to fully love me. At age eighteen, I ended up in a relationship with a guy who was known to be a heroin addict; when I look back now, I think a part of me thought I could save him from himself. Again, with no understanding that there is only One true Saviour who was longing to do the same for me, too. I soon found out I was pregnant, and my doctor knew of our drug use and recommended an abortion. She even called the clinic to make the appointment for me. She failed to mention the potential for immense guilt and shame that might sideswipe me and forever alter the fabric of my story, and four days later—that is exactly what happened. I could not stop the darkness from overwhelming my thoughts, my heart, and my body. All I wanted was to numb the pain. A few short weeks later, I tried heroin for the first time. They told me it was a small amount for a first-time user and all I recall was vomiting and not thinking or feeling anything. I wanted more. Within two weeks, I was using it every day; caught up in a cycle I would not know how to name for the next six years. A cycle that led me to become the opposite of everything I had ever imagined being—caught up in crime, mixing with dangerous people, stealing from family and friends, growing, and selling drugs and eventually, a prostitute. Selling my body and my soul to strangers for my next fix, over and over and over. Again, lost, confused, and alone.

One night my mom showed up at the illegal brothel I was working in and told me she loved me and that she would always be there for me. She told me she had been praying to God to save me from myself and that she had always believed I had been born for a purpose. She wept. I felt nothing. Not long after her visit and after six years of surviving with a consuming drug addiction, at the age of twenty-four, I decided to try to get help; and this time, I meant it. I had tried so many other things— crystals, acupuncture, meditation, astrology, Buddhism, to name a few, but nothing worked, and I desperately wanted to be clean. I had no idea that there was a huge difference between being clean and being free; but I knew if I didn't get clean, I was going to die. I sought help from a doctor who worked with drug addicts and had a good success rate of people getting off drugs and staying off them. I sat in his waiting room, with my faithful Mom by my side; not fully grasping how I had ended up here but with a deep sense that this was somehow my turning point. When we sat down in his office, he asked me my drug history and why I wanted to be clean. I told him that for the first time in over six years, I was scared I was going to die. He looked me in the eye and said, "I don't think drugs are your problem, I think your problem is you have a hole in your soul that only Jesus can fill." I was horrified and very quickly told him what he could do with *his Jesus*. He told me if I wanted his help, I needed to go to rehab. Three days later, when I entered rehab, I experienced the gift of belonging for the first time in a very long time. I signed all the paperwork and committed to the program. However, that night, some people came over and did a Bible Study and sat around singing songs about Jesus. I was angry, I felt side-swiped, yet again and even though I rejected their kindness and care, they kept showing up for me and speaking hope and life into my future. I endured their program, the visitors, and their continual hope for my breakthrough but on Sundays, I would sit outside the church hall and blow my cigarette smoke in the building to annoy them until one Sunday, it was pouring rain, and I had no choice but to go inside the building.

On that day, August the 15th 1999, I sat through a message I did not understand with my head, and I felt a holy tugging on my heart. At the end of the service, I responded to the altar call and gave my broken heart to Jesus Christ. In that very moment, He met me right where I was, and just as I was, and He loved me back to life with His glorious grace and redeeming love. And thus, my own redemption story began. Just like Mary Magdalene, I knew I had been set free so I could live free indeed, with a deep and profound knowing that the deep loneliness and fear of my future, which had been with me for all of my days, had been forever quenched by a love unlike any other love. A holy and healing love that transformed me from the inside out. With one touch, one encounter with His presence, I was born again, Spirit-filled, and He set my feet on the narrow way and not once since that moment have I ever walked alone. I fell completely in love with Jesus and His Word and immersed myself in it all through the gift of worship music with every waking hour. I knew I had been completely forgiven and set free. I told everybody who would listen, and many who would not. When I stopped cursing and cussing every second word, people also knew I had been touched and a little revolution of His love overtook the rehab home, with many others giving their hearts and lives to Jesus Christ, too. I, like Mary, wanted my life to count for something. I wanted to live in a way that was living proof to all of those around me that no matter who we are or what we have done, or what has kept us bound, that nothing can stop His love from setting us free, freed to be fruitful. Being set free by Jesus Christ changes you, from the inside out. In the many years since that day, I have had the honour and privilege of lavishing my love from Him onto others by partnering with the purposes of Heaven in a myriad of ways. I have raised three daughters with His wisdom and guidance, I have written books that tell of His goodness and His power to set people truly free, I have spoken around the world telling others of His love through the power of redemption, I founded and ran a charity to come alongside other women who were trapped just like I was, and I studied counselling, so that I could better support those wanting to process their past, live fully in their present, and be future focused. Because, just like Mary, I love Him with my whole life, and I want the world to know that *he who the Son sets free IS free indeed* (John 8:36, NIV). My past is not my future, and I know that now.

Mary Magdalene lived a life that humanized the Word of God, revealed the love of God, and let each one of us know that He is devoted to walk alongside us for all of our days, in and through it all, He is the Constant One. She remained steadfast and faithful to the very end.

I want to be like Mary. Don't you?

Lot's Wife

Leandria Benton-Tsosie, *46 years old*

"Remember Lot's wife." Luke 17:32

"For I know the plans I have for you," declares the Lord, *"plans to prosper you and not to harm you, plans to give you hope and a future"* Jeremiah 29:11, NIV.

Speaking of Lot's wife, Genesis 19:26 tells us, *"But his wife looked back from behind him, and she became a pillar of salt."* Like Lot's wife, I, too, looked back. It was not with desire as Lot's wife had but it was out of the inability to see what good could be before me. I now know that when I am walking with God, I can be assured that the vision He gives isn't some far-fetched, out-of-reach idea, but it's a marking to show the next goal line. But it wasn't always like that.

I grew up on a Native American reservation in Northern California. I have seen that living in the past can be an honor by keeping our identities alive, but it can also be one of the most destructive mindsets a person can have. I wonder what exactly was in the mind of Lot's wife when she longingly looked back at the city of Sodom. Was she thinking of the places where her children took their first steps? Was she thinking of the special place she liked to visit with her husband? If her family was already with her while leaving the city, what else would there be? What was it that would make her long for such a wicked place to look back for even a second?

The reality is that things don't always have to make sense for us to believe it. I remember being a young mother living with a man who continually cheated on me over the span of eleven years. This was at a particularly vulnerable time in my life because my mother had died suddenly, and I hadn't yet dealt with the grief. Apart from the infidelity, he was good to me. I say that because to some, they will be astounded that I could actually say that. I mean, if you're in a relationship with someone, what else is there if you aren't faithful to one another? But to others who may have gone through this, or are currently going through this, the thought process may be familiar. It wasn't physical abuse or the like that kept me there but it was the thinking of past times we had shared that were great and the belief that it could be that way again. It had become a way of life for me. I can clearly remember the times I found out, by a phone call, through family members, and even pictures. Each time it happened, I would cry and begin to clean my house from top to bottom, trying to find some control in my life. I couldn't control his thoughts, whereabouts, or emotions but the furniture arrangement, the color scheme of the linens, I could control that. And I did.

I knew I deserved better than the relationship I was in. I knew of the goals and aspirations that the Lord instilled in me, but I couldn't see myself there. When I did think of completely ending the relationship, I would have thoughts of shame that this person cheated on me. The Lord really had to minister to me on this in order to break out of this mindset. I cried out to the Lord many times alone because I was unable to tell my family because I knew what they would tell me. I think back now and I can see that it is absolutely absurd that I would be ashamed that I was cheated on, but that is how Satan works.

Throughout my life, I have learned of Satan's many devices by them being used on me. The things that Satan uses in our lives to blind us and keep us there is everything and anything he can possibly use. He isn't a foe that fights fair and he isn't too proud to hit below the belt. It doesn't always have to make sense for us to believe it and Satan counts on that.

But, each time I cried out in prayer, the Lord would strengthen me a little more. It took many tears and many conversations with God for me to finally wrap my head around the fact that the infidelity that took place had no bearing on the person that I am. What began with a hope for a healthy and productive relationship ended with multiple devices used to hinder and delay what God had for me. I can see that now. And what was one person's problem quickly became my problem when I was outside God's plan.

One of the things I have learned about God is that the quicker I run to Him, the sooner I bring Him into my situation, He is faithful to give me the grace and help I need. It's Him who can peel back the blinds from our eyes so that we can see what He would have for us. I came to know His plans for my life through prayer and reading His Word. Knowing the will of God for my life has enabled me to walk in His blessings. I think about that also when I think of Lot's wife. The Lord commanded them to not look back.

The Lord's desire was for them to be obedient because He knew that destruction would come. And so it is with us, when we walk outside the will of God, He knows what will come. It is especially important for us to know the will of God for our lives if we have a calling on our lives. The enemy, Satan, he will know who we are before we know who we are and he will hurl those fiery darts hot and heavy. If we are outside of God, it may delay us for a time but the quicker we run to God, the Holy Spirit is quick to lead us back to the right path.

There were so many times in my life I believed something erroneously. I choose now to believe wholeheartedly in the inerrant truth of God's Word, even when it's outside my natural ability of understanding. I'm speaking of believing God for the good things He has for us because Psalm 68:19 tells us that *He loads us with benefits every day*. Sometimes, it's easier to believe in God's goodness for someone else but not quite as easy to believe it for ourselves. He is the God that knows the end from the beginning, choose to trust that there is hope and a good future that is in store for us. Do not be held captive by the situation, the circumstances, or the familiar, allow God to lead us out. I speak from just one woman's perspective but I pray the Lord shines light on every shadow and dark place in our lives, so that we may know His plans for us. Don't look back!

"I pray that the eyes of your heart may be enlightened in order that you may know the hope to which he has called you, the riches of his glorious inheritance to his holy people" Ephesians 1:18, NIV.

Salome

Dee McGinnis, *70 years young*

"Now when the Sabbath was past, Mary Magdalene, Mary the mother of
James, and Salome bought spices, that they might come and anoint Him."
Mark 16:1

W ho was Salome? Have you heard of her in the Bible? You
may be saying, "Never heard of her," or wasn't she...? The
truth is, I did not know that there were two Salome's mentioned in the Bible. We are learning together my friend. I
have the distinct privilege and honor to be sharing about
Salome, the wife of Zebedee and mother of James and John. AHHH
YES, those two brothers who end up being Jesus's disciples. Okay Dee,
what do you have to say about her?

First, can you imagine being married to a fisherman in the days of
Jesus? How were the living conditions, especially with two boys close in
age? Her husband Zebedee seemed to have been a man of some position
in a city called Capernaum. According to Luke 5:4, Zebedee had two
boats and according to Mark 1:20, they also had *"hired servants"*.
Salome would of course be a woman who kept and prepared for Shabbat
every week. Shabbat headscarves, candlesticks, and spice boxes (in
Hebrew called *besamin*). These may seem like little things, but in many
households, these are precious heirlooms, just like the Mezuzah. A

mezuzah is of biblical origin and therefore carries great weight. *"And you shall inscribe them on the doorposts (mezuzot) of our house and on your gates"* see Deuteronomy 6:9, 11:20, *What is to be inscribed? Divine instruction* is very clear: *"The words that I shall tell you this day": that you shall love your God, believe only in Him, keep His commandments, and pass all of this on to your children."*

Hence, a mezuzah has come to refer also to the parchment, or *klaf*, on which the verses of the Torah are inscribed (Deuteronomy 6:4-9, 11; 13-21). Mezuzah refers as well to the case, or container, in which the parchment is enclosed. A mezuzah serves two functions: Every time you enter or leave, the mezuzah reminds you that you have a covenant with God; second, the mezuzah serves as a symbol to everyone else that this particular dwelling is constituted as a Jewish household, operating by a special set of rules, rituals, and beliefs. *Would you be able to pass down traditions from one generation to the next?* Can't you just see Salome with her husband Zebedee, and sons James and John sitting near a wooden table? She had prepared the meal, along with the challah bread (from scratch), and then straightened her head covering and finally lit the candles? Then, they prayed and she could sit and rest. The lighting of the candles during Shabbat was so important that wayfaring Jews keep portable candlesticks on them on their sojourns, so that they may honor God through the blessing over the candles.

Whether at home or on the road, the lighting of the Sabbath lights is a visual reminder to keep Shabbat and honor God. Salome would probably go to the market and look at the fresh fruits, vegetables, leg of lamb, or eggs and pick up the wine for the meals. No car, or Uber, no Insta-Cart, no delivery service, just her feet and homemade bags to carry things in. Maybe the fun was in the haggling and the great exercise of the walks. I imagine that the little town she lived in was pretty quiet when Rome was not asserting their authority or collecting taxes. That would be until Jesus came on the scene!

What would you really do if you knew that the Messiah was alive, in your village? Would you doubt? Would you scoff? Who would you question to find out if indeed it was the Messiah?

SALOME

Stop and think for a minute. You are in your hometown, regular events happening, you know almost everyone, you travel to Jerusalem three times a year together to celebrate the festivals, and your normal discussions are about herbs, children, your animals, and your husband's latest catch in the sea and then one day, your husband comes home and tells you that the Messiah has come and both your boys are going to follow Him? Would you be as faithful as Salome? Would you want to question Jesus? Well, she did and would, more to come on that. Would you want to ask your husband if he was crazy to let them go? Would you question your sanity? You had prayed your prayers as a good Jewish woman for the Messiah to come and save your people, then you hear that not only is He here, but He wants your sons to follow Him? Who among us would have that kind of faith or belief? Salome did! She knew her boys, now young men, had flaws, shortcomings, and yet how proud would you be as a mother to know that your sons were called by Jesus, despite some of their weaknesses. How did she really know Jesus was the Messiah at the time of their being called to join Him?

Mark 2:3-11 recounts what took place in her little neighborhood. She lived in Capernaum where someone's home had the roof torn off to let in a paralyzed man whom Jesus healed.

"... four men arrived carrying a paralyzed man on a mat. They couldn't bring him to Jesus because of the crowd, so they dug a hole through the roof above his head. Then they lowered the man on his mat, right down in front of Jesus. Seeing their faith, Jesus said to the paralyzed man, "My child, your sins are forgiven." But some of the teachers of religious law who were sitting there thought to themselves, "What is he saying? This is blasphemy! Only God can forgive sins!" Jesus knew immediately what they were thinking, so he asked them, "Why do you question this in your hearts? Is it easier to say to the paralyzed man 'Your sins are forgiven,' or 'Stand up, pick up your mat, and walk'? So I will prove to you that the Son of Man has the authority on earth to forgive sins." Then Jesus turned to the paralyzed man and said, "Stand up, pick up your mat, and go home!"

Salome was a woman of belief I would say, a woman of bravery, a woman of valor. Is that the way your friends and family would describe you?

Now, let us recall that both John and James, her sons, had to have had strong personalities. We learn this when Jesus Himself gave them the nickname the *Sons of Thunder*. See Mark 3:17. Not only did Jesus know and love these two brothers, but He also used their strength to lay a great foundation of service and love, despite their shortcomings. Before we go any further, let's talk for a second about the surprise that may register on Salome's face when she found out that thousands of years in the future, they were calling one of her sons James, not Jacob. You see, Jacob and James are variants of the same root and stem from the Hebrew name *Yaaqob*(יַעֲקֹב) which is translated as "Jacob" throughout the Old Testament (Genesis 25, 29). In Mark 3:17, Complete Jewish Bible states: *"Ya'akov Ben-Zavdai and Yochanan, Ya'akov's brother —to them he gave the name "B'nei-Regesh" (that is, "Thunderers")."*

In the Tree of Life Version, Mark 3:17 says: *"...to Jacob and his brother John, the sons of Zebedee, He gave the name Boanerges, which is Sons of Thunder."*

Okay, so now Salome's sons are called Sons of Thunder… so maybe the thought of thousands of years later being called James is not such a surprise. Salome was a follower of Jesus, she got to hear Him speak and possibly perform miracles, and she might have made meals for Him. Salome was bold and courageous! When Jesus finished talking to a crowd about the parable of the day's labors, (see Matthew 20) He was on the way to Jerusalem with the twelve and said,

"We are now going up to Yerushalayim, where the Son of Man will be handed over to the head cohanim and Torah teachers. They will sentence him to death and turn him over to the Goyim, who will jeer at him, beat him, and execute him on a stake as a criminal. But on the third day, he will be raised."

This incredibly strong and bold woman went so far as to *intercede* for her sons, with them in tow with her. *Who do you intercede for?*

Now in person, with her boys, she asks the Messiah Himself a question. (Courage) Now this was after the Parable of the day laborers. In Matthew 20:20, she comes up to Jesus kneeling down and begging for a favor – Jesus asks, "What do you want ?" Can you even conceive

SALOME

what a *bold and beautiful heart* this mother had for her grown children, for their future?

Matthew 20:20-23 Complete Jewish Bible states: *"Then Zavdai's (Zebedee's) sons came to Yeshua with their mother (Salome). She bowed down, begging a favor from him. He said to her, "What do you want?" She replied, "Promise that when you become king, these two sons of mine may sit, one on your right and the other on your left." But Yeshua answered, "You people don't know what you are asking. Can you drink the cup that I am about to drink?" They said to him, "We can." He said to them, "Yes, you will drink my cup. But to sit on my right and on my left is not mine to give, it is for those for whom my Father has prepared it."*

Salome was so *devoted* that when her own sons had turned away, she remained with Jesus's mother Mary, and Mary of Magdala during the horrendous scene, there had to have been an unruly crowd crucifixion (See Mark 15:40-41). I cannot imagine, can you? Being an onlooker with your Messiah being crucified? I am crying just thinking about this as I type. Salome was also mentioned in Mark 16:1, which establishes that she was one of the women who appeared at Jesus' tomb. So, she continued to care for Jesus after His death with a *willingness*, along with Mary of Magdala and Mary, the mother of Jesus had bought spices so that they might go and anoint and cover a day's old body, Jesus' body. What a burden and honor. What a privilege and yet such grief must have been with her. After years of devotion to Jesus, she was chosen to be one of the few women to find the empty tomb. An angel gave her the news that Jesus had risen from the dead.

Salome was known for being a devoted mother and follower of Jesus. Together with her husband, Zebedee, they raised two faithful sons, chosen to be among Christ's disciples. Salome *interceded* for her sons, asking for seated positions to the left and right of Jesus.

I am grateful to have learned so much about Salome. My life, indeed, is blessed knowing more about this woman who lived in a community with other faithful and obedient followers when Jesus walked the Earth.

Achsah

Dr. Mary Iles, *64 years young*

"So Othniel the son of Kenaz, the brother of Caleb, took it; and he gave
him Achsah his daughter as wife." Joshua 15:7

Reflecting on the Scriptures, particularly Judges 1:14-15 and
Numbers 13, the narratives hold profound lessons echoing
throughout generations. Achsah's story resonates deeply within
me, echoing the depth of human experience intertwined with
divine purpose.

*"Then it happened that when she came to him, she incited him to ask
her father for a field. Then later, she dismounted from her donkey, and
Caleb said to her, "What do you want?" She said to him, "Give me a
blessing: since you have given me the land of the Negev, give me springs
of water also." So, Caleb gave her the upper springs and the lower
springs"* Judges 1:14-15, NKJV.

In Numbers 13, the leaders sent to scout the land painted contrasting
pictures. Most returned with tales of daunting giants, portraying the
Israelites as insignificant grasshoppers. Yet, Joshua and Caleb saw
differently—a land flowing with milk and honey, teeming with promise.
Their faith set them apart. They didn't merely see challenges; they

envisioned God's abundance so much so they brought back large grapes carried on a branch they'd cut down, with pomegranates and figs.

Joshua was a warrior himself and his best friend Caleb, I would call him a leg soldier, both men believed in God and had a relationship with him. They were not afraid to take the land. So, after Moses' death, Joshua was appointed by God to lead the people into the promise land, and according to Moses, they (Joshua and Caleb) would be rewarded for their bravery. Moses had allotted land to each tribe. After forty years of battles and pioneering, the tribes of Israel were settling down into the new land. Many battles were conquered yet there was still one enemy left. Caleb, from the tribe of Judah, put out a petition saying, *"To the one who attacks Kiriath Sepher and takes it, I will give my daughter Achsah as his wife"* Judges 1:12 NKJV.

Despite numerous victories, one challenge remained. Caleb pledged his daughter Achsah's hand to whoever conquered Kiriath Sepher. Achsah's choices, seemingly mundane, resonated spiritually. Like her, I've found unexpected challenges shaping my journey. Achsah's tale mirrors the nuanced fabric of our lives. Born into privilege, my early years exuded abundance and limitless possibilities. However, life took a turn, transplanting me into a challenging environment. It was a transition from opulence to the struggles of the ghetto—a jarring shift that shaped my perception of the world. The transition to a new school, relegating me back to a lower grade, left an indelible mark—a suffocating feeling akin to a land devoid of water. Achsah's boldness resonates; she sought more to nurture her family and land.

Jesus invites us to ask, seek, and knock. However, we must ponder our use of what we already possess. Rejections, like those I faced, often conceal blessings. Jeremiah 1:4-5 is a beacon—God's foreknowledge and purpose for us predate our existence. Dr. Myles Munroe's profound analogy of holding a forest within our grasp resonates deeply. It mirrors the potential and the rich reservoir of possibilities that often lie untapped within us.

His quote, "We hold a forest in our hands, not a seed; for every seed it represents a forest; and every tree there is a fruit or a flower seed in them; and every seed has a tree that has fruit that will in turn produce its kind" (Munroe, 2021).

Personally, if Maya Angelou stopped writing before she discovered she had more inside, her piece on "Phenomenal Woman" would have never changed the lives of so many women. Suppose Ruth decided not to follow her mother–in–law Naomi back to Bethlehem, she would never have met Boaz who birthed Jesse who birthed King David. We are more than we realize. Personalities like Maya Angelou and Ruth reveal the untapped potential within us. Apostle Paul tells us we can come boldly to the throne of God and with confidence. I believe this is us today as we use the stories of the Bible to feed us when we need the joy, the love, and/or the peace of God. When we need the strength to endure the journey to get to the other side. Life's rejections taught valuable lessons, guiding me to understand the influence of closed doors, transforming apparent setbacks into stepping stones. Closed doors were not the end but a passage to discovered potential.

My grandmother instilled a giving spirit in me at a tender age. Eventually, I understood and embraced Jesus's giving on the cross which was a pivotal moment akin to finding my spring. Achsah's boldness, inspired by Joshua and Caleb, echoes in our ability to draw strength from biblical narratives.

God's ways surpass ours; He urges us to move to His rhythm. We own nothing; all is a gift from God. Achsah's request, though bold, aligned with God's plan. Similarly, our potential is inherent since God formed us.

Many carry emotional burdens like depression, influenced by others' opinions. Identifying our truths allows us to seek spiritual nourishment. There was a man (Jesus) coming who simply understood the challenges of physical damage. Like the woman who sought healing, acknowledging our need for more leads to transformation. This woman said, "If I could only just get through the crowd, I don't care how dumb it looks, I don't care how stupid it looks, I don't care how many people I have to go through, if I have to crawl on my knees to get to this man, I will do the necessary at all costs because I need more.

At the end of the story, the woman touches the hem of His garment, and she is made whole. How many of you today, right now as you're reading the pages of my story, are saying to yourself, "I need more"? You are in a dry place. Is the place you're in producing what you want? Is the place that you're in difficult to see your way through? Is that place you are in causing you to feel like you're a barren woman without children? And you're saying *if I could just touch His* garment!!! You need more love; you need more of Jesus's open arms. You need more peace, more compassion, more spiritual strength? If I could leave you with anything, I will say to you as you're coming to the end of my story, go to the Father and ask Him for the spring of water, so that your roots will be planted deep. I had no clue that coming off of drugs, surviving domestic abuse, and weathering the storms in my life in due season that my land would be prosperous. If I had stayed in the mentality of someone else's s opinion of how my destiny should be, I do not believe I would have had the courage to write these pages.

I, too, faced struggles but found strength in Joshua 1:9-11 (NKJV), *"Have I not commanded you? Be strong and of good courage; do not be afraid, nor be dismayed, for the Lord your God is with you wherever you go." Then Joshua commanded the officers of the people, saying, "Pass through the camp and command the people, saying, 'Prepare provisions for yourselves, for within three days you will cross over this Jordan, to go in to possess the land which the Lord your God is giving you to possess."*

My family provided so much support, shaping my resilience. Jesus's love strengthened my boldness; I am a product of His compassion. My dad was my biggest fan. My grandmother, who raised me, was my nurturer. My mother (both natural and stepmom) gave quiet love. In it all, they encouraged me to be the best at whatever I did. Discovering my potential is much greater today than where I was years ago. My abuse was the product of someone else's dysfunction. The storms in my life were because of my choices. My boldness is because of Jesus's love. Love is the product of God's heart. Achsah asked for more land so she could survive her environment. She needed the springs of water to produce an inheritance for her family lineage. Never limit your self-value by the negative thoughts of someone else. Our real intelligence is not studied, it is discerned. Our own greatness is not from our image of our strength, but from the strength of the Almighty and wonderful God. You are an amazing person, who has amazing dreams, visions, and blueprints of destiny on the inside.

Be true to God when you look in the mirror, be true to self when doubt comes, be true self in your struggles, and be true to self when you hear the voice of God. Do not let things or life hold you from being all you can and should be. God has given us this new piece of land. Over the course of my journey to become, I had to see God change some of the most life threating moments to celebration.

Maybe you're saying I don't see the land/my water; I don't see how God can use me. I am not like Achsah or you, Dr. Mary.

Can I tell you, I was not always this person you are reading about, but what I did do, I got still, got tired, and not that I heard so much of an audible voice. I will say, it was through the scriptures and presence of God, and His love, that picked me up from that dark and dry place.

Our intelligence isn't merely academic; it's discernment. Embrace God's truth, reject doubt, and honor His voice. We mustn't let life hinder our potential; God's love sustains and transforms us.

The story of Joshua and Caleb provided the reservoir of courage that seeped into Achsah's veins. Similarly, through biblical narratives, we draw strength, joy, and perseverance. Just as the Red Sea parted for the Israelites, there's a divine intervention waiting to unfold amidst our trials.

Psalms 114 reads that when the Red Sea felt the presence of God, it stood up. I might say, the water became a wall and Israel walked on dry ground.

Eve

Samantha Grandson, *43 years old*

"And Adam called his wife's name Eve, because she was the mother of all living." Genesis 3:20

Eve is known as the first female, the mother of all living human creations. She was also Adam's wife. In the King James Version of the Holy Bible, the book of Genesis, Eve was created by God (Yahweh) by taking her from the rib of Adam, to be his wife (Help Mate).

"And the Lord God said, 'It is not good that man should be alone: I will make him an help meet for him'" Genesis 2:18.

"And the Lord God caused a deep sleep to fall upon Adam, and he slept: and he took one of his ribs, and closed up the flesh instead thereof: and the rib, which the Lord God had taken from man, made be a woman, and brought her unto the man. And Adam said, This is now bone of my bones, and flesh of my flesh: she shall be called Woman, because she was taken out of Man. Therefore shall a man leave his father and mother, and shall cleave unto his wife: and they shall be one flesh" Genesis 2:21-24.

As I think of Eve and all the many things that she represents, the one thing that stood out the most, or should I say the one thing that relates to me, is how God created her from the rib of Adam. This is exactly how I felt when I married my husband in 2019. I felt like God had created me all over again and from the rib of my husband. It felt like I was created just for him. As I reflect over my life, I begin to realize that I have been in many relationships, some good and some not so good. However, none made me feel the way I did the day I married my husband. The feeling reminded me of the day I gave my life to Christ. I felt born again, renewed, and revived. I felt like a WOMAN.

I was twelve years old when I began to get intimate with boys and men. I had always desired older men and later on in my life, I learned why. As a little girl around the age of five, I was molested by a family member. A much older person at that. I heard before that most people desire what they encounter first. For many years, older men were my desire. As a young girl, I never understood what was happening to me. Honestly, I thought it was supposed to happen because he was my family and he loved me, so that is what he told me. Sex became a part of my life at a very young age. I would be in relationships for years and sex, most of the time, was my main focus. If we weren't having sex, I didn't feel needed, wanted, or loved. I always thought the only thing that would keep a man happy was sex. It was not the cooking, cleaning, and taking care of the kids. It was the sex for me, at least that's what I believed. Not only was that something that I believed, it's something that we were taught in the African American Community. I would always hear older women and my friends say things like, "Girl, if you don't give it to him, (meaning sex) someone else will." It was like they were teaching you that sex is the only thing that would keep a man. Nevertheless, I believed it.

I met my husband working at a Rehabilitation center. He was coming there to have physical therapy. I remember sitting at my desk and in walks this very young, slim handsome man. He was wearing a black Adidas sweatsuit with red lines on the side, and red and black Adidas shoes with a matching cap. I looked and it was like a movie. Immediately, I heard the Holy Spirit say (That's him). I knew exactly what *That's him* meant. After about three appointments, he and I exchanged numbers, then we began dating. Sex was definitely hot and heavy early on. Remember, that's what I knew to do. As time went on, he began to say things like, *we don't always have to have sex, or sex is not everything in a relationship*. I can't lie, it did make me feel some kind of way at first. I began to think the worst, as if he wasn't into me anymore. Clearly, that was not the case.

My husband is the first man that taught me sex is not the most important thing in a relationship. I had to learn to build my relationship on things that will last. However, it still took years for me to understand how to do that. I would get angry with him when he did not want to have sex. It made me feel like he did not want me or was interested in someone else. (My oh my, how the enemy plays on the mind). He would say, "Baby, the sex is not going anywhere, we have a life time together." But coming from my background and what I believed, it did not sit well with me for a long time. I was so used to just giving myself away, not honoring my body. I used to hear older people say, *take care of your body, that's your temple*. In my head, I would tell myself, this is my body and I do what I want with it.

"Do you not know ye not that your body is the temple of the Holy Ghost which is in you, which ye have of God, and ye are not your own" 1 Corinthians 6:19.

Now that I am older, mature, and saved by grace, I understand and sometimes I wish I could get a do over. But trials and tribulations are just lessons learned to make you a better person. I thank God because now, I can truly say that I value my temple. I am a wife, a mother of three beautiful children, and a grandmother of one little boy. I teach my children; well, young adults now, to value themselves, not to give their bodies away. To keep God first and trust Him in all that they do.

Anna

Josephine L. Martin, *70 years young*

"Now there was one, Anna, a prophetess, the daughter of Phanuel, of the tribe of Asher. She was of a great age, and had lived with a husband seven years from her virginity." Luke 2:36

I n the Book of Luke (2:36-52), this woman named Anna was on a special assignment from The Lord God Almighty. God had in mind to send The Messiah and This Messiah was His Son, Jesus Christ. In order for this Messiah to be born, someone had to pray for this to happen, and this someone was Anna. So, Anna was in the school of preparation, all hindrances had to be removed, her husband had to be removed, and no offspring was given unto her. All the emotional baggage had to be removed, including the sorrow and mourning for her earthly husband. As she turned to the lover of her soul (The Jehovah Jireh) her provider, He gave her beauty for ashes. Meaning, He took her sorrow (ashes) and He gave her joy, and so Anna started to love on the Lord night and day, by praying, fasting, and worshiping God.

"To all who mourn in Israel, he will give a crown of beauty for ashes, a joyous blessing instead of mourning, festive praise instead of despair" Isaiah 61:3.

Anna in the Book of Luke was married for seven years to a husband and had no children all her life on this Earth. After the death of her earthly spouse, she was mourning. To mourn in those days was to be covered in all black and be secluded from all others of society. Could you imagine having lost your earthly spouse and now to be isolated, or shut in, for a long period of time. That was sorrow on top of sorrow and sorrow upon sorrow which added to her current mourning. Being in that dark place for a long period of time can be detrimental to one's mental health and wellbeing.

This type of grief is not good for the body. Combine this with no physical food, which has nutrients for the body. Also emotionally, this is devastating to the mind, one is down and cannot think right or one might lack concentration, the ability to think right. Whatever sorrow you are going through, the Lord doesn't want you to stay there for a long period of time in that sorrow. He just wants you to visit that place and come out as quickly as possible, because that's your training ground and not your staying ground. Don't you camp there permanently but temporarily, because the Lord doesn't want you to haul this emotional baggage around. God wants us to come out of life's sorrow, and sadness. These are heavy burdens to carry. Jesus already took the burden of grief, sorrow, and sadness at Calvary's Cross. The Bible says burdens are lifted at Calvary's Cross, Christ is our burden bearer. So, let us leave all these distractions at the feet of Jesus Christ.

Anna had to make that decision. I am going to come out from this place of sorrow that I find myself in, it is not doing me any good, and those around me either. Women of God, I want to encourage you that unless you make a decision to come out from whatever sorrow you are going through, that thing, or that problem, makes you go backward and not forward. Remember, the Lord did not give us backward feet to go backward, but to go forward. So remember, backward never but forward forever. Jesus is not coming back to go to Calvary's Cross. He is not coming to go backward, that is to bear our sin again. So, Jesus is not coming back to be afflicted a second time by mankind, but He is coming back with power when every knee shall bow before Him and every tongue will confess that Jesus is Lord. Behold, He comes riding on a horse, and not riding on a donkey because riding on the donkey showed His humility. Riding on a horse shows his power, Hallelujah, (Amen).

Anna probably said to herself, *no more of this sorrow, no more mourning, no more grief and no more sadness in my life*. I am making a decision today. I am going to live for my God and I am going to be an instrument for Him, and a vessel for Him here on Earth. Anna could have chosen to marry a second time (husband), maybe it might have worked out, not having any sorrow for the second marriage. But she did not take that chance a second time. I am sure Anna did not want to have sorrow a second time in her life, she did not want to go that route again. She had her share of sorrow, enough is enough. Out of that marriage there was no seed, but sorrow and grief, and the marriage was short lived (seven years). But she took a chance with The Lord God Almighty and her life was not the same. Anna decided to live the rest of her life for the Lord and so she decided to live in the Temple of God praying, worshiping, and fasting night and day. The thing that caught my eye is how she did that night and day. I said to myself, how did she do that? My, my, night and day. Maybe, God knew that her husband was going to be a hindrance when it comes to her prayer, fasting, and worshiping God. This right here was going to be a problem to her earthly husband, there was going to be jealousy when Anna, his wife, was giving all her attention to the Lord, like praying, fasting, and worshiping The Lord night and day. The Holy Spirit revealed something to me a long time ago and He brings it back to my memory again as I am writing this devotional exhortation. The Bible says when you marry, you have to devote your time to one another. 1 Corinthians 7:39 says, *"A woman is bound to her husband as long as he lives."*

This right here is a conflict of interest, unless you both agreed to serve The Lord together, with no strife, no jealousy, no discord, no malice, no backstabbing. These are all fruits of the flesh, and these fleshly concerns will show up if there is no oneness, no unity, and no togetherness in Jesus' Name. I know there are a lot of women who are in this dilemma as I am writing. Women are threatened by their spouses if they serve The Lord, almost like Anna, and they will divorce them. Women cannot pray in their homes, cannot sing when they are taking a shower, are told they are praying too loud, and women are locked out from their homes. Some women are threatened to the extent that they cannot focus on the things of the Lord, but I encourage you, don't give up. Help is on the way. He said I will not leave you and I will not forsake you especially when it's about Him. (Amen).

The Lord God knew Anna's heart and so He had to protect her *"Anointing."* He also knew she was going to be an instrument by praying for the coming Messiah, and worshiping Him. In order to do what Anna had done, it takes killing the flesh, sacrificing the flesh, and dying to the flesh. She also lived in the Temple of God. My fellow brothers and sisters in Christ, what a sacrifice Anna made for us, are we willing to make that sacrifice today for our Lord and Saviour?

I encourage all of us women to seek the Lord when it comes to marriage, much less first, second, third, fourth, fifth, six, and seventh marriages like the woman at the well. Don't let the devil set you up with his obnoxious trap. Whatever situation you are in, seek the Lord's guidance. Today, there are many in such situations, they are not enjoying but enduring, and The Lord does not want that for us, it grieves the Holy Spirit. So, let us continue to do what we can for the Lord and leave the rest to Him. Just be an instrument for Christ like Anna was and you will become a dynamite for Christ like Anna.

Anna decided to serve the Lord wholeheartedly; therefore, her service for The Lord was not short-lived like her marriage of seven years. The Word of God says that Anna served The Lord until she was eighty four (84) years old. What a blessing, our God is a blesser if only we will be obedient and faithful unto Him. Anna was able to hold baby Jesus whom she was praying for. In Luke 2:39, it says, *"So when they had performed all things according to the law of the Lord, they returned to Galilee, to their own city, Nazareth."* The Priest, or Priests, wanted someone else to bless baby Jesus, but the Lord had to set the record straight by letting them know that there was one who was praying for the child Jesus night and day, you don't know about her, I know about her, and let her (Anna) bless the child Jesus. You might be that Anna that nobody knows about, but God knows you. As I am writing, I am jumping for joy, God will reward you for your labor of love for Him. The suffering you are going through, the rejection, isolation, the gang up, the sickness, and the loneliness, God will reward you in due time, just like He rewarded Anna with a long and happy life in Him. I would not trade my God for anything else in this world. So, don't give up on the Lord, because He will not give up on you. Amen. He did not give up on Saul when Saul was on Satan's commission. Jesus came into the picture and changed Satan's commission to His (Jesus') commission.

I chose Anna because of what the Lord has brought me through. I purposed in my heart that I am grateful, thankful, and appreciative of Him to deliver me, which no man could have done but my God. And so I choose to serve My King, My God, My Strength, and My Good Shepherd with praises, worship, thanksgiving, prayer, and fasting. I thought I could not have done what Anna did. But when I purpose in my heart to do it, My Lord and My God granted me my desire to serve Him night and day. So, if Anna was one woman who prayed for our Messiah and it came into fruition, what if all the women of God do that. Women of God, we will turn the world upside down and Satan would have no clue what happened to him!

Rachel

LaTrina Cartwright, *42 years old*

"Then God remembered Rachel, and God listened to her and opened her womb." Genesis 30:22

THEN GOD REMEMBERED—Her Lot & Legacy

I can recall the night that I began researching the life of Rachel. I remember crying uncontrollably. Her story was so painful to read, but it also made me wrestle with the divine providence of God. I had to take a moment to digest all that she had to go through. Let's take a stroll down memory lane.

While on her way to the well to feed her flock, Rachel runs into a man by the name of Jacob, who would change her life forever. Rachel runs home to tell her father of their long-lost family. Rachel's father, Laban, is Jacob's uncle, which makes them cousins. Laban is thrilled to have Jacob come live with him and help tend to the flock. This is a cause for celebration. In Genesis 29, we come to know that Jacob falls in love with Rachel and agrees to serve Laban for seven years in order to take Rachel as his wife. After serving Laban for the years agreed upon, Laban tricks Jacob and arranges for him to marry his eldest daughter, Leah, instead.

Oh, the scandal… I wondered how Rachel must have felt when she learned that the man she loved was now wed to her sister and that her father had deceived them both.

Laban now promises Jacob that he can marry Rachel if he serves another seven years. Jacob agrees and marries Rachel a week after his marriage to Leah. Jacob fulfilled the fourteen years of service to Laban in order to be with Rachel. Everything seems fine until Leah begins bearing children. Rachel asks, "What about me?" Jacob responds with "Am I God, He's the one who kept you from having children?" My modern mind said, "How dare he say that to her." She must have felt so fragile and grief-ridden. But I can recall a time in my life when I, too, wanted results from my husband that only God could fulfill.

Imagine being promised a husband, but your sister gets to marry him. Then, your sister taunts you because she's able to bear his children and you are barren. Imagine the many nights of longings and crying. The Bible tells us that Jacob LOVED Rachel. Imagine that despite knowing that you're loved, the thing that you desire the most has been withheld from you. Disappointment clouded any consolation that Jacob's love could bring. Then finally, the Bible says in Genesis 30:22, "THEN GOD REMEMBERED."

Oh, what a feeling when God remembers the tears you've cried, the long sufferings, the heartbreaks… Rachel never asks for this life, but she must endure its challenges and oppositions. God looked upon Rachel and remembered. Just as he had done for Jacob's mother, Rebekah (Isaac) in Genesis 25:21. Just as he'd done for Jacob's grandmother, Sarah (Abraham) in Genesis 21:1-2. Just as He had done for Hannah who was a descendant of Rachel in 1 Samuel 1:19-2, to name a few. He never forgot about them. One day time stood still, and God remembered. Oh, how I rejoiced to know that He was still writing my story.

Long story short, Rachel conceived Joseph and then Benjamin. We all know the story of Joseph with the coat of many colors. Joseph that was sold into slavery by his brothers, but in the end proclaimed, *"But as for you, you meant evil against me; but God meant it for good, in order to bring it about as it is this day, to save many people alive"* (Genesis

50:20, NKJV). He quoted the sentiments of Rachel's life. Many things were meant for evil, but God turned it around for her good. Through her bloodline, God positioned Joseph to save the children of Israel. Her lot preserved her legacy.

I remember facing a situation in my life that left me in such a broken place. In 2015, my child was sexually assaulted by an elder at a church. The elder was well known and protected by this church. My husband and I chose to report and pursue criminal charges against this leader. This decision came with such devastation and major repercussions because we thought the church would stand with us. Oh, we were sadly mistaken. We both worked at the church, so we eventually lost our finances, our church family, and the enemy tried to destroy our faith. Over the course of seven years, I remember the grief, the anguish, the bargaining with God to restore my joy, to revive my spirit, and mend my broken heart. One day, on December 11, 2022, *God Remembered*. He remembered my pain and my shame. He sent restoration to my house.

Time and time again, we keep witnessing God's unfailing love for us and His promise that He would never leave us nor forsake us, and that He will uphold us with His righteous right hand (Hebrews 13:5-6 and Isaiah 41:10). I encourage you to not give up… the day is going to come when *God Remembers You…*

Lydia of Thyatira

Sherrell Wallace, *48 years old*

"One of them was Lydia from Thyatira, a merchant of expensive purple cloth, who worshiped God. As she listened to us, the Lord opened her heart, and she accepted what Paul was saying." Acts 16:14

We are introduced to Lydia in Acts chapter 16. Paul was on his second missionary journey being divinely led by the Holy Spirit. *"Paul and Silas traveled through the area of Phrygia and Galatia because the Holy Spirit had prevented them from preaching the word in the province of Asia at that time. Then coming to the borders of Mysia, they headed north for the province of Bithynia, but again the spirit of Jesus did not allow them to go there. So instead, they went on through Mysia to seaport of Troas. That night Paul had a vision: A man from Macedonia in northern Greece was standing there pleading with him, "Come over to Macedonia and help us!" So we decided to leave for Macedonia at once, having concluded that God was calling us to preach the Good News there"* Acts 16:6-10.

After following the Holy Spirit's leading into Macedonia a few verses later, Paul made his first evangelistic contact with a group of women. In verse 14, we are introduced to Lydia from Thyatira, a merchant of expensive purple cloth, who worshiped God. I remember as a child having a love for fashion. I would spend hours drawing outfits with my colored pencils and crayons. I would spend hours flipping through fashion magazines and looking at the beautiful clothing, shoes, and jewelry. I would daydream about becoming a fashion designer and helping women look beautiful and feel confident. I imagined the fabulous life the women in these magazines must have, wearing those amazing outfits. In my imagination, they had the perfect life both inside and out.

One day in the fifth grade, I had this overwhelming feeling almost like an audible voice that said, "One day, you're going to do something great!" I remember immediately thinking, "I am going to be a fashion designer," but then, I immediately thought, "but that's not anything great." Right then and there, while sitting at my desk in the fifth grade, I declared to myself that I was going to be a fashion designer/social worker.

I grew up going to church and even got baptized at a young age, but it wouldn't be til much later in life that I would truly realize that the overwhelming feeling I had, the feeling that was so overwhelming it almost sounded like an audible voice, was the voice of God telling me my future. It wouldn't be til many years later at the age of thirty-two that I would begin my journey of pursuing God's plan for my life. In the Fall of 2007, I was laying across my bed in tears. I felt so empty and thought, *there has to be more to life than this*. I had a family, complete with two beautiful daughters, Telsey, 9 and Hallie, 4, their dad, and me. We had all the material things like a house and two cars and the things we needed and wanted. I had the American dream, but I still felt like something was missing.

While I was laying across my bed in tears the phone rang. When I picked it up, it was my Aunt Sherryl who lived in Minnesota. She was my favorite aunt, I had looked up to her my whole life. She was beautiful with a joyful personality and an amazing sense of style. She inspired me to fall in love with fashion at a young age.

She called to say that God had put it in her heart to tell me that "He had a plan for my life that was bigger and better than anything I could dream or imagine." Tears streamed down my cheeks because I felt what she was saying was true. My mind immediately went back to the fifth grade when I had that overwhelming feeling that one day I was going to do something great! She then told me that the only way I would find out His plan was to start going back to church. The next day was Sunday, so I got my two daughters ready and we went to a church that I had visited as a teenager with my cousin. This church was very small, almost like a house, but I was determined to find out this plan God had for me, so I decided I was going to go to church that day no matter where it was. One thing my aunt told me before we got off the phone was that I would know I was in the right church when I felt like the pastor was speaking directly to me. When I got to the church, the people were very welcoming and greeted us with smiles and hugs. When church service was over, the pastor was very friendly with a big smile and came up to me and my girls joking and laughing. I felt so much love and joy that I decided to go back the following Sunday. On that second Sunday, I remember the pastor had everyone turn to a page in the Bible and he read a scripture that I had never heard before.

"For I know the plans I have for you," declares the Lord, "plans to prosper you and not to harm you, plans to give you hope and a future" Jeremiah 29:11.

At that moment, I got chills all over my body because I felt like the pastor was speaking directly to me, just like my aunt had said. I knew I was in the right church. I kept going to church faithfully, excited to find out the plan God had for my life. The more I kept going to church, the more I discovered. I was discovering who God was and how much He loved me, I was learning about Jesus and how He died on the cross for me, and I was learning about the Holy Spirit that Jesus gave us here on Earth to dwell in us to lead, comfort, and guide us (Read John 14:16).

I discovered that the Holy Spirit that led Paul and Silas to Macedonia was the same Holy Spirit that led me to that church and wanted to lead me to God's plan for my life. I kept going to church faithfully, excited to find out the plan and the purpose God had for my life. Little did I know, a few months later, my life would drastically change. On Father's Day of 2008, my fifteen year relationship ended, and I found myself single with two little girls, ages five and ten and pregnant with our third daughter on the way. I thought to myself, what kind of plan is this!!??

I ended up losing my house to foreclosure and being on government assistance to help me care for my daughters. Government assistance brought me great relief, but also great shame. I had worked my entire life and never depended on the government. One day in church, the pastor asked if anyone wanted to surrender their life to Christ. I had been going to church but had not fully surrendered my life. It was almost as if an invisible force pulled me up out of my seat and I stood up and surrendered my heart fully to God. A couple months later on June 6th of 2010, I got baptized again. I began to rely on God like never before. I prayed and gave all my problems to Him. I saw God make a way when there seemed to be no way. Money came from the most surprising and unexpected places and my bills got paid, and car repairs and other needs were taken care of. My faith in Christ was growing stronger.

"You saw me before I was born. Every day of my life was recorded in your book. Every moment was laid out before a single day had passed" Psalm 139:16.

What attracted me to Lydia was her occupation as a woman who dealt with purple cloth. She was a business woman in the fashion industry. Something I aspired to be. But her life is so much more powerful than her occupation. God used her for His purpose and plans to share the Good News. Lydia was a business woman with an open heart, an open mind, and an open door. She was the first convert to the Christian faith from the city of Philippi. Lydia of Thyatira is widely known as a fellow disciple of the Gospel that provided a resting place for Paul and other disciples, and possibly financed the travels of those traveling from city to city.

"She and her household were baptized, and she asked us to be her guests. "If you agree that I am a true believer in the Lord," she said, "come and stay at my home." And she urged us until we agreed" Acts 16:15.

Every night, I diligently asked God what He wanted me to do with my life. I was seeking Him with my whole heart and He was revealing Himself to me.

"If you look for me wholeheartedly, you will find me" Jeremiah 29:13.

At the age of thirty-two, God started reminding me of my childhood dreams. I realized that my talents, abilities, gifts, and interests were given to me by Him. He had given me a love for fashion. When I started pursuing God's plan for my life, I was searching for His hand, but as I kept searching, I began to see His face. I began to see not only His love for me, but His love for others. I was learning God's plan for us is not ours alone. When we seek out God's plan for ourselves, we are also activating His plan for others. Our dreams and desires are somehow connected to someone else's dreams and desires.

On May 29th, 2011,while getting ready for church, I was watching the TBN Christian station. The Pastor on this particular program was talking about how Christians needed to live from the inside out. He said we needed to come out of the closet and share what God has done in our life. I felt guilty while listening to His sermon because God had done so much for me but I really wasn't telling anyone about it except for maybe people in my church. As this pastor was giving his sermon, I started envisioning a T-shirt that was inside out and I visualized people asking me why my shirt was inside out, and I saw myself giving them a little card with my testimony on it. That was the day my business "Living Inside Out Apparel" was inspired. I started to take action on this vision God gave me. Step by step, God started bringing me provision. Miraculously, I received everything I needed to bring His vision into reality, the equipment to make the T-shirts, the resources to create my logo, and creating the testimony cards. God gave me the vision and made the provision all in the same year.

God will move Heaven and Earth, moon and stars, time and space, to reconcile us back to Hs family. God's sovereignty is a necessary aspect of our evangelism. God opens hearts and does the conversion work. It's up to us to hear Him, and cast out the seed of His work into the world through our words, actions, and talents, and abilities and gifts. If others respond, we know God has opened their heart; if not, we can rest that God has another plan for their life. Other people started living out the faith Lydia brought to them. Trust and rest in God's sovereign timing. He has a plan and purpose for your life that is bigger and better than anything you could ever imagine.

Martha

Melissa Edman, *38 years old*

"But Martha was distracted with much serving, and she approached Him and said, "Lord, do You not care that my sister has left me to serve alone? Therefore tell her to help me." Luke 10:40

When I was asked to choose a woman in the Bible that I could relate to, I didn't search long. Martha was one I knew I could relate to. She is first mentioned in Luke, and she was busy. She is busy doing exactly what I thought was my entire purpose, serving. It all began for me at my church. I heard a story from a church member of her experience on a mission trip. It set my heart on fire to serve Jesus in this way. I started praying and searching for mission trips that I could do with my nine year old son. A friend came to visit me one day and she told me about YWAM (Youth With a Mission). I applied and was accepted into a YWAM in Colorado Springs, Colorado. God miraculously provided for my son and I to go. We were looking at three months in Colorado Springs to do classes and then three months in the field, which turned out to be Thailand for my son and me.

In our time in Colorado and Thailand, we experienced cleansing, healing, and so much learning. After that, my heart to serve God kept growing and I felt I was on the right road. Once we left YWAM, we began to search for a place to serve long term. I felt God was calling us to Bethlehem, South Africa. We were supposed to be there for two years but our time there was cut short. We came back to the States after six months. I still had the urge to serve God overseas but one day, my son asked me if we could stop and just stay home. He wanted to have a normal life. I said yes and that's when our life took a different turn. I was no longer looking to serve God overseas and we settled into a "normal" life.

The next ten years go by in a flash. I continued trying my best to follow God and do what I thought He wanted. In that time, I met my husband, we got married, and had a little girl together. My desire to serve overseas was buried beneath worries that I wasn't doing enough for God. That I needed to be serving Him somehow and I wasn't. I was just living a "normal life." I just knew somehow I did something wrong or made a wrong decision and that's why I haven't been able to go back to "serving God" the way I thought I should. In all those years of living my life and waiting to go back to serving God, not once did I stop and say, "Jesus, what happened?" Not once did I rest long enough to hear an answer. I was so focused on serving, serving, serving.

I was Martha. And just like Martha, Jesus had to bring me back to what the real focus should be, Him! *"But the Lord answered her, "Martha, Martha, you are anxious and troubled about many things, but one thing is necessary. Mary has chosen the good portion, which will not be taken away from her"* (Luke 10:41-42). Mary wanted to sit at Jesus' feet and listen. She was focused on relationship, where Martha was focused on works. I also was a woman focused on works. I was so focused on it that I made it an idol. God had to bring me to my knees in order to show me that I was putting works before my relationship with Him. When I started out with a heart on fire to serve God, I wasn't wrong. I just allowed the works to become more important. When my son asked for us to stay home and I thought I had made the wrong choice, it was God leading me away from missions for a time. He did not want me to find purpose in that, He wanted me to find my purpose in Him and Him alone.

As a little girl, I only wanted to be a wife and mother. That was my sole yearning for so long. When I went into missions, if God had let me continue to do missions with the mind frame I was in, that works is more important, and given me the gift of being a wife and mother during that time, I would have felt like I earned that gift.

Ephesians 2: 8-9 says, *"For by grace you have been saved through faith; and that not of yourselves, it is the gift of God; not as a result of works, so that no one may boast."*

God will not share His glory. He wanted to show His glory in my life and He wasn't going to let me take it from Him. In all of this, we must know even when our life is not going the way we think it should, God is intricately planning out the details of our lives in love and grace. He's more in control than we think and it's always for good and for His glory! And if we put anything before a relationship with God, He will do what must be done to bring us back to Him. It may look like things aren't making sense or it may seem like life is so far from what you thought it would be, but in reality, it's our sovereign Lord lovingly guiding us to where we can go deeper with Him. To a deeper relationship that causes us to want to do works for Him out of love for Him!

The Woman
at the Well

Sarah Hampton, *26 years old*

"A woman of Samaria came to draw water. Jesus said to her,
"Give Me a drink." John 4:7

When you recognize where the enemy came in, you become stronger when you let your weakness marry God's strength. When influences creep in, they can create demonic thorns that get stuck in your soul. What is your soul? Your mind, will, and emotions. This can dilute and twist your thoughts, manipulate your emotions, and disrupt God's plan for your life. This is a dangerous place for the one that does not have a saved soul. This lost soul is not only living a dark life but has allowed the thorns to get stuck in their soul with no way out. This dark place is no home for His children to live. Their souls are homeless. This requires the power of God to touch them in such a way to set this captive free. The world is craving that which is beyond. There is that within humanity which is calling out for the supernatural. If they can taste and see the powers of the dark realm, they can handle tasting and seeing the powers of the Holy one. It is time for the Church to give the way out.

When devils try to strike back again, you have a history of the transformation to show you have once encountered this before, coming out of that attack God entrusted you to go through. Why?

Much like the Samaritan woman and the radical encounter at the well, she came to the well in the heat of the day one way but ran into the city to the faces of her enemies another way. Set free from all the strongholds that captured her in bondage, deceiving her very eternity to ever face Christ the way she was, and by the words "I am He," all evil was taken away in an instant. I am sure when she went into the city, she was despised and hated. They tried deceiving her of her salvation. "She is not worthy enough. Now here she is talking about Christ that Messiah is here and there is coming a day, which is now already here, we can worship God anywhere by Spirit and Truth. This woman is unclean, who is she to encounter Christ!"

I believe one of the evilest things the enemy can rob you of is taking you to an old, stale version of you making you think you belong there rather than this new creation, set apart, sanctified, purified, holy, righteous, redeemed from the curse, and separated for such a time as this. Read *1 Corinthians 6:11* and *1 Corinthians 1:30*. Your salvation is secured in Him, not in man. Man's validation is invalid when you already have the validation from your Creator, your Heavenly Father.

The woman in Samaria came to the well at noon, the hottest hour of the day. Why did she go at this time? Why didn't she go early in the morning? People from the town usually came early in the morning to avoid the heat. She kept away from the people claiming they all hated her, despised her, disrespected her, and called her a prostitute, making her feel unworthy, insecure, and full of shame. This amount of persecution making you believe a lie of the enemy gives Satan access, causing strongholds to build up.

Jesus said, *"If you knew the generosity of God and who I am, you would be asking me for a drink, and I would give you fresh, living water"* John 4:10.

The Samaritan woman could not even see who she was talking with. Even after Jesus gave her the very truth she needed to hear with the words:

"Whoever drinks of this water will thirst again, but whoever drinks of the water that I shall give him will never thirst. But the water that I shall give him will become in him a fountain of water springing up into everlasting life" John 4:13-14.

Something shifted to catch her attention that had her command, *"Sir, give me this water, that I may not thirst, nor come here to draw."* John 4:15

What she missed is what I missed. Unless I knew Him, I would continue to thirst for the natural over and over convinced it will save or fix me or fill my void I was trying so desperately to fill. When Jesus is saying, *"I hold the answer Daughter, thirst no more!"*

Strongholds cause you to have a spirit of deception. *This spirit of deception is after your spiritual sight.*

She perceived Him as a prophet rather than the Messiah with a word coming to her with the very next verse, *"Go, call your husband, and come here,"* Jesus said in John 4:16.

The woman answered and said, *"I have no husband." Jesus said to her, "You have well said, 'I have no husband,' for you have had five husbands, and the one whom you now have is not your husband; in that you spoke truly"* John 4:17-18. There was something in these marriages that were not fulfilling for her. Even the one she was living with was not her husband, yet she still needed to fulfill something from him. As if she was thirsting for him rather than *Him.*

Spirit of God preserves the Spirit filled, born again believer from any attack against you. When the pressure comes, we press back; we have the belt of truth and the shield of faith quenching every fiery dart against the deceptive attacks of the enemy. See *James 1:27, Galatians 3:13, John 15:19,* and *Psalm 91:10-12.*

It has no power against you. What shifted the atmosphere into the Samaritan woman first believing He is a prophet to who He actually is, was after the woman said, *"I know that Messiah is coming" (who is called Christ). "When He comes, He will tell us all things"* John 4:25. Jesus responded with the words that broke history from that moment on and wrecked her heart from the mindset that once held many strongholds in her soul, in John 4:26, which states: *"I am He."* Catch the revelation in this! "I am He." It is equivalent of saying, "In the name of Jesus."

How many of us know when we say, "in the name of Jesus," darkness must flee, the sick must be healed, demons are casted out, strongholds are demolished, and sight of deceit is opened. There is a reason the Word says to *"resist the devil and he will flee."* NOT the Holy Spirit. The Word says, *"do not grieve the Holy Spirit,"* Ephesians 4:30.

The anointing carries a fire that not only burns hotter than that which comes against you, but it also breaks every yoke. It tears down walls that have been built up for way too long. It plucks up every demonic thorn we call strongholds in your soul that have been pressed in deeper the more you do not take care of it, much like a splinter that has not been taken care of. It is now infected. The anointing can take away and burn up hurts and offense that took place and be thrown into the lake of fire for eternity. When the woman left in freedom and God set her ablaze allowing her to go into the city saying to all, she said, *"... come see a man who told me all things that I ever did. Could this be the Christ? They went out of the city and came to Him"* John 4:29-30.

Strongholds were being demolished and vision became clear in sight believing she truly had just met the coming Christ that is now here—MESSIAH! JESUS! Something had to have broken within the woman, something was demolished within her the moment He said, "I am He," there was power. For her to run into the town despite their hatred and disbelief. The word of knowledge giving her a way out of the darkness into the light worshipping in Spirit and in Truth, the city now knows who has come!

Declare this over your life any time the spirit of deception tries to run rampant within your life, strongholds take place, any time people, spirits, situations, circumstances, or demonic influences try to steal away your salvation: "I threaten the enemy for I know I am here to subdue the dark kingdoms to restrain him and release God's Kingdom upon the Earth in Jesus' name. It is my God given right and Spiritual authority to take hold of the demonic witchcraft like spirits and bind them straight back to hell and loosen a fresh supernatural boldness upon my life. I bind the spirit of witchcraft planting any tricks of deceit. I bind the spirit of deception and loosen the spirit of truth. I bind and pluck out every demonic thorn causing strongholds to build up like walls around me for way too long. I bind and take authority over any demonic thoughts and demented dreams not from you Father. Spirit of death be gone in Jesus' name. I take authority over the spirit of suicide. I loosen a heavenly freedom from all bondage I have been held captive. I bind any revolving door in the form of a witchcraft grip, in any place, not allowing me to leave. For Your will for my life is to destroy the works of the devil and do the works for the Kingdom. My strength does not come from the world or man, but by the power and the fire of the Holy Spirit which revives within me to know what to do, when to do it, how to do it, and where to do it, in Jesus' name, Amen!"

Susanna

Adrienne Greene, *72 years young*

"And it came to pass afterward, that he went throughout every city and village, preaching and showing the glad tidings of the kingdom of God: and the twelve were with him, And certain women, who had been healed of evil spirits and infirmities, Mary called Magdalene, out of whom, went seven demons and Joanna the wife of Chuza Herod's steward, and Susanna, and many others, who ministered unto him of their substance."
Luke 8:1-3

While there is not much written about this faithful steward, one thing is for certain, she was a lover of our Lord and Savior, Jesus Christ. And for sure, there is enough written about her to impact the lives of those who are determined to give their ALL to Him. Scripture has it that Susanna was one of MANY which ministered out of their personal substance to sustain our Lord Jesus Christ. He did not lack anything, as she provided. The Bible says in Luke 7:47, *"Therefore I say unto thee, her sins, which are many, are forgiven, for she love much. But to whom little is forgiven, the same loveth little."* Hence, is my similarity to the life of Susanna. I was healed of many infirmities and delivered of many demonic spirits.

My past is one who came from a divided household. My parents separated while I was at a very young and tender age. My memories are that of total negativity as there were often very bitter arguments and physical battles between my parents. My mother eventually had a breakdown and was admitted to a psychiatric ward. After a short stay with a beloved and (sorely missed) aunt, myself and two siblings were placed in foster care. Trauma left an indelible mark in my childhood years as I tried to process life on a daily basis. As God, in His sovereignty, did see to it that we were placed in a most loving home with Christian foster parents. Still, the longing for a birth parent is painful to say the least. As the oldest sibling, I had to constantly show strength for my sister and brother. Feelings of abandonment I am sure haunted them both, without verbalizing.

Years begin to pass and my sister and I, gifted to sing, began to sing in *night clubs*, much to my foster mother's chagrin. We were young. She raised us in church. But she caved in by peer pressure. Her beliefs as to our "*age*" were opposed by many in the "village" even the local church. And so opened the "gate" where the demonic spirits began entering, unbeknownst to us. I was now facing high school graduation. Sadly, my foster mother passed a few weeks before graduation. Trauma again. I was devastated. What next, is all I could think of.

After graduation, we were now placed back into the care of my birth father and his girlfriend. This transition rocked me and my siblings' world. A life we were not used to was now our daily confrontation. Personality differences among other issues. During this time, we found out my birth mother had passed. We did not know. Too long of a story. But of course, trauma again. A few months into this transition, my sister and myself began to sing in nightclubs again. The entertainment field became our way of life. Exciting even more now since we were transitioned from country living (Long Island, New York) closer to city life. Producers, a little fame, and meeting people was our excitement. And now, the introduction to drugs and alcohol.

During this time with my father, I also met who would become my husband. We married and had one child from this union. My marriage failed after three years. I was still trying to figure out who I was and what I wanted to do with the rest of my life.

Soon after this separation, my sister and I began to embark on a very long and dark road. Her with the hard drugs, me with the alcohol. Long nights at clubs began to take a toll. As years passed, the drinking escalated and soon, I found myself needing to drink daily. Even as I relocated from New York to California, hoping that would somehow help the problem, it only worsened. California wrought more drinking and night clubs, as my aunt was also a night club jazz singer and pulled me into the world. Alcohol began to take a toll on my health and social life. By this time, my sister was heavy into drugs. We were both trying to cover the deep pain with a band aid that did not work. My brother was trying to cope as best he could. We were both out of the home and doing our own thing.

During these times of darkness, I remember the Lord *always* placing someone in my path to tell me about the good news of Jesus. Of course, I was not ready to surrender, although beaten down by this life I was living. By the time I returned from California, I was emotionally, physically, and spiritually spent. There was no life in me anymore to speak of. I moved in with another dear and sorely missed aunt and her husband. Months went by and she realized the condition I was in due to alcohol abuse. And here goes the beginning of my deliverance from many demons.

One day when my aunt and uncle were out of the house, I remember I began to drink again. My uncle also drank, so alcohol was readily available. I was a black out drinker so there were times I did not remember things that people would tell me I did or said. I do remember this certain day, the Lord chose as my day of deliverance. I turned the radio on and surfed until I found a Christian station. I have no idea how I even found it, but the Lord does. There was a woman on a prayer line and gave the prayer number to call for prayer. I dialed the number. I do not remember anything after dialing, but hearing her begin to pray. I am here this day to tell the world, I have NEVER TOUCHED ALCOHOL AGAIN since then. God delivered me that day from the demon of alcohol. And the journey continued from 1981 to 1983 when I gave my life COMPLETELY to the Lord and have never looked back. I was filled with the Holy Spirit and Jesus and I have been on a love journey since then.

Yes, I can attest that those who are forgiven *MUCH* love *MUCH*. Where would I be without the Lord? I shudder to think of the consequences. I can think of many instances I could have been dead in my sins and trespasses, but *GOD* in His tender mercies. By His stripes, I have been made every whit whole. By His blood, I have been set free to praise and worship the King. I have been delivered to snatch as many that would say *I will*, from the pits of hell. This is my testimony and determination. My desire is to be an effective disciple of Christ, partnering with those of the Body of Christ to tear the devil's kingdom down. My *substance* is His as was Susanna's, as He supplies ALL that we need.

WHOSOEVER shall call upon the name of the Lord, SHALL BE SAVED. And oh yes, my sister was also beautifully saved before the Lord took her home to be with HIM. No better place to be. Matthew 10:5-8 says, "FREELY ye have received FREELY give." (Read in its entirety.) This is my forever MOTTO for life. What HE has done for me, I will take it to the world, just as Susanna did, along with all the women that were healed, delivered, and set free from their own evil spirits and infirmities.

TO GOD BE ALL THE GLORY FOR THE GREAT THINGS HE HAS DONE!

The Woman

with the Alabaster Box

Marcia Blair, *49 years old*

"And being in Bethany at the house of Simon the leper, as He sat at the table, a woman came having an alabaster flask of very costly oil of spikenard. Then she broke the flask and poured it on His head." Mark 14:3

I have always delt with shame. It has always been a dark cloud that hovered over me. I was ashamed of being adopted. I was ashamed of some of the houses we lived in growing up. We didn't have much money, so I was ashamed of the clothes and shoes I wore because they were affordable for my parents. I felt ashamed when I got bad grades. Some of us heard growing up, "you ought to be ashamed of yourself," or "shame on you." Believe it or not, these types of statements, even if said by someone who loved you, can follow us for a lifetime and impact the way we interact with God. What ends up happening is every time we do something "wrong," it produces shame. Especially as followers of Jesus, when we don't measure up or we believe to have let Jesus down by our mistakes and flaws, we can sometimes feel shame. The good news is the love of Jesus is unconditional. Remember what happened with Adam and Eve in the Garden of Eden? After they sinned against God, they felt shame. The guilt of sin caused shame. And because of the shame, they hid from God. But even it that, God, rich in mercy, provided clothing for them (Genesis 3:21). Yes, God wants us to be obedient. Yes, God wants us to repent when we are not. But God never wants us to feel ashamed. We cannot allow guilt to transform into shame and allow shame to influence us to hide ourselves from God.

There have been several times on my Christian journey that I have made mistakes, big and small. If I'm being honest, there have been some occasions where I've allowed the guilt of my sins and shortcomings to put me in a position where I tried to hide myself from God; much like Adam and Eve did. I found myself in a place of isolation. Not only isolating from family and friends, but even worse, isolating myself from God. You may think, "how can you isolate from God?" We know God is omnipresent. He's always there. David asks in Psalm 137, *"Where can I go from your Spirit?"* I've heard many a testimony where the sentiment is, "I left God, but God never left me." That, too, could be a testimony of mine. I have had broken fellowship with God the Father because of guilt and shame. In my mind, I had let God down and because of that, I wasn't worthy of His love. I wasn't deserving of His grace. I wasn't justified for His mercy. Oh, what a lie that was. An *alabaster box* moment is what changed it all.

Let's look to the Woman with the Alabaster Box whose story is told in Mark 14:3-9 and Luke 7:36-50. What I love most about this unnamed woman is she did not allow shame to keep her from a chance encounter with Jesus. She did not allow shame to cause her to hide herself from Jesus. She ran to Jesus, not from Him. Luke 7:37-38 (NIV) gives this account of the woman with the alabaster box.

"A woman in that town who lived a sinful life learned that Jesus was eating at the Pharisee's house, so she came there with an alabaster jar of perfume. As she stood behind him at his feet weeping, she began to wet his feet with her tears. Then she wiped them with her hair, kissed them and poured perfume on them."

This woman was known to be a sinful woman. I can imagine the shame she could've felt not only in the presence of Jesus, but also in the presence of those who had likely been critical and judgmental of her because of her sinfulness. However, unlike Adam and Eve and unlike me, she didn't hide. She came forward.

This woman, despite her sins, had a pure heart of worship. The Bible does not account for any words spoken by the woman, just worship through deed and in action. She wept at the feet of Jesus, kissed His feet, and wiped them with her hair. She was not in the least bit concerned with what others thought as she poured out her worship unto the Lord. She then breaks the seal of the alabaster box and allowed the sweet fragrance of its contents to permeate the room as she anointed Jesus (Luke 7:38). In those days, the breaking of an alabaster box was a big deal. An alabaster box was a vessel with a narrow neck filled with costly perfume called Spikenard. Spikenard symbolized the very best in ancient cultures. This likely was the woman's most valuable possession. It was the best she had to offer, and she willingly poured it out as an act of sincere worship. Once the neck of the alabaster box was broken, there was no going back. The vessel could not be resealed. The entire contents would have to be poured out. As she poured all of herself out at the feet of Jesus, she also poured out all of her most valuable possession. She gave her all, in more ways than one.

Although she was giving her very best to Jesus, ridicule and anger still rose up against her by those in the home who witnessed what she was doing. She was challenged with questions of the logic of breaking the alabaster box and pouring out this expensive perfume. She was met with anger for "wasting" the perfume. Mark 3:4-5 (NIV) says, *"Some of those present were saying indignantly to one another, "Why this waste of perfume? It could have been sold for more than a year's wages and the money given to the poor. "And they rebuked her harshly."* Even being faced with this ridicule and rebuke, she did not let it disturb her focus to pour her whole self out in worship to Jesus.

Rest assured there will be times when those around you will not understand your worship. Those around you may not understand your sacrifices to Jesus. There may be people around you that know your past sins who may turn their nose up or raise a brow at you. There have been times where I have been hesitant or reluctant to give God my full worship because of my surroundings or environment. I was fearful of being misjudged or criticized. I have learned to take on the boldness and courage of the *Woman with the Alabaster Box* and not let anyone or anything stand in the way of my full worship to a worthy God.

We can glean a lot from this woman. Never allow shame to keep you from the feet of Jesus and always offer to Him the best of what you possess. Never allow the chatter of those around you to disturb your worship to God. I can imagine this woman tuning everyone out in the room, and it was just her and Jesus. She wasn't concerned with what others thought or said. The only thing she was concerned with was honoring and worshipping Jesus. Her mind and heart were focused on that one thing. And Jesus welcomed and received her sacrifice and her worship.

We should be encouraged in knowing there is not one that is so dirty that Jesus would say go away from Me. There is not one so dirty that Jesus would say I don't love you. Nothing disqualifies you from the love of Jesus. Run to Him, not from Him. Hide in Him, not from Him. Jesus accepts our pure, genuine worship.

I believe it's also noteworthy to see how this short story of the *Woman with the Alabaster Box* ends according to Mark 14:6-9 (NIV). It says, *"Leave her alone," said Jesus. "Why are you bothering her? She has done a beautiful thing to me. The poor you will always have with you, and you can help them any time you want. But you will not always have me. She did what she could. She poured perfume on my body beforehand to prepare for my burial. Truly I tell you, wherever the gospel is preached throughout the world, what she has done will also be told, in memory of her."* Not only did Jesus receive her worship, but He also rebuked those who ridiculed her. When you are doing a righteous and pure thing, Jesus will always cover and protect you.

Jesus is worthy of our all. Jesus is worthy of our most sacred worship. What is most valuable to you that you could offer as a sacrifice of worship to the Lord? What is your *alabaster box*?

Joanna

Laurie Hook, *62 years old*

"… and Joanna the wife of Chuza, Herod's steward, and Susanna, and many others who provided for Him from their substance." Luke 8:3

Greetings, I had never considered the beginnings of women's ministry, nor had I considered writing about a woman of the Bible whom I might parallel my life with. Initially, I had chosen two other women both who were already chosen. So, I asked the Spirit what now, and He led my finger down the list of names, and it stopped at *Joanna*, "Who the heck was Joanna?" My mom hadn't heard of her. My bestie hadn't heard of her, and I certainly had over-looked her. Aunt Lenora says she was part of the corporation. Score another for the Holy Spirit, so with great excitement, I began researching this blessed woman of God.

I texted Deborah and revealed this was more like a book report than a discovery of the similarities of a Bible character and me. That's alright though, because God knowledge is God's healing in my soul… and blow my mind He did. I believe I needed the distraction as I am learning to be much more. I also discovered how ignorant I am as the Journey of my mother's life is ending. It's been a slow and disheartening year and a half, exhausting to say the least. but with Him, I know I am an Over-comer! (1 John:1-5).

Joanna is only mentioned twice in the Bible: the first time, married to Chuza, manager in the household of Herod Antipas, ruler of Galilee. (I began to freak out as I discovered Herod would be the one who mocked and dressed Jesus with a royal robe before sending Him back to Pilate) Luke 23:6-12. The second time was at the tomb, the morning of the Resurrection. She was one of the first women on the scene. We are told that Joanna was a woman of means and connection. Yet this Jewish woman had an unmentioned disease, or infirmity, that led her to Jesus (Luke 8:3, Matthew 9:35). I can imagine after she was healed she might have ran to her husband to tell him of the astonishing news. There was no mention of his reaction, and I wonder if he was relaying messages to Herod that "this Jesus healed my wife," but I can imagine Joanna's proclamation to those around her saying, "This man Jesus has healed me of my infirmity and I will follow Him, for my life is been changed."

Was Chuza exuberant over his wife's healing, surprised, flabbergasted even? Did he send her off with joy—leave the palace and fulfill your heart's desire. I choose to believe God softened his heart, he choose to fill her purse and loved her On Her Way. Joanna became a part of Jesus' inner circle of women, Mary, Mother of Jesus, Mary, the mother of James and John, Mary Magdalene, Mary Clopas, Susanna, Salome, and other women, there for every extraordinary event their walk with Jesus entailed. They ministered to Jesus and the disciples through their own substance. Johanna's journey with the disciples was approximately two years. Women were not given much respect in the man's world, but Jesus made certain He was communicating, instructing, listening, directing, and including the women, whose hearts and minds He touched and healed, those of great faith, bold women who heard and saw the miracles Jesus performed. I can only imagine the transformation of physical, spiritual, and self-healing walking with Jesus, it must have been like extravagant love, so humbling, overwhelming, unimaginable, restorative love. The only thing Joanna could do was follow to learn, listen, care for, and serve the leaders of the pack and other women who were chosen to follow the Messiah along the way. Whew! Hold it now, I'm just a farm girl. How could I possibly find commonality in life with a woman of means, a leader in her household, and an influencer of those in her universe? Well, why not me?

JOANNA

I was sixteen when I asked Jesus into my heart walking down a country dirt road with another who had done the same. I wish I remembered who she was so I could thank her for the best decision I could make. I was baptized as a baby into the Lutheran faith, and went to a Lutheran school for a couple of years. What a blessing to have the foundation started in my youth (Proverbs 22:6). I learned of Jesus, that He loved me and He died for me... the beginnings of a love like none other. But I did not understand this love. My youth was filled with contradictions of what love was. My father had convinced me he was god. I grew up, believing God was the authority figure I could never talk to, religion and human word took root. God was too big and all power-ful, but I did know that *Jesus loves me for the Bible tells me so,* my go to song when I'm faced with life's personal difficulties. I can do all things according to Philippians 4:13. Coming up, I saw the women of the Church were the organizers, preparers in the works of the Church. I do not remember their conversations of Jesus' mighty love, or of the Holy Spirit.

Bummer, as I age, I realize how religious teachings are so hit and miss. I was, though a part of those who served and I loved being a helper volunteering where needed, watching the ladies work in unison learning how to strengthen my talents and gifts. They were an unknown, but I was happy helper who is always learning how to take instruction and completing tasks, elevating those that needed a hand and bringing peace to certain situations. It's amazing what a smile can do. Growing up, the eldest of five, these early exposures of how to be organized, preparing tables, cooking, cleaning, and organizing time became the foundation for caring for my siblings. Truly, after researching Joanna, I felt as though she could've been the elder, or mentor, I certainly could have served for or with.

Joanna, how amazing your time must've been traveling with the Teacher, the sermons you heard, the miracles you saw, I can only imagine the reverence when He taught the Beatitudes, Matthew 5:7. I can imagine you serving, greeting, and surely listening when Jesus spoke. Oh, the wonder of this peace. My favorite story is in Luke 9:13, the miracle of feeding the multitude with a lunch from a small boy. Oh, I wonder what became of him; he gave what he had, and watched how it became more than enough. Joanna, I can just imagine you were filled with incredible joy as the bread and the fish fed 5000 along with the women and children, then to see the 12 baskets return full. I can imagine the glee and laughter... did you sing the praises of Jesus, thanking God as you went?

So many amazing things. Being the wife of Chuza, did you recognize the men who followed and relayed messages to Herod of what Jesus was doing. I'm sure he was aware of your healing, and your conviction to serving our Lord. Were you aware of the chief priests and scribes desire to kill Jesus, Matthew 26:1-5? I believe you could've known they followed Jesus and His followers everywhere! Joanna, you witnessed so much joy and pain, laughter and tears, love and loss. As Jesus' final hours were increasingly intense, I assume you and the other women surely were working with Peter and John as they carried out instructions from Jesus, every moment preset by God, what you must've heard, and would have come to understand. The last supper would be the last time you would see Him, not knowing the hell our Savior was about to endure, Matthew 26:56, then the disciples forsook Him and fled.

How alarming it must've been when the news of Jesus' arrest was proclaimed, the frantic search, finding Jesus tired, mocked, ridiculed, and abused, but you, the women, stayed. What a horror you all witnessed. What inner strength you and other women had, bonded together in service of Jesus, and yet unable to do anything for Him. You all followed Jesus to the Cross, never letting Him out of sight, yet having to remain in control. Even on the Cross, He spoke to you, "Do not weep for me" Luke 23:27-31. What perseverance... that is love beyond understanding. Only John was at the Cross with you all. You showed how, as women, we are far stronger than I was ever taught. We can stand and overcome, even when it seems all hope is lost. Even after watching Jesus' death, you and the women disciples kept your composure as caregivers. I can imagine the tears as you cared for Jesus' body and prepared it with myrrh and aloe supplied by Nicodemus, John 19:39-40. What an honor!

As a caregiver and a daughter, I, too, have been honored with preparing the physical body for being received. I pray your tears helped to heal your heart. But then came Sunday morning. Oh how you all must have had so many emotions that Resurrection morning. Mary Magdalene, You, Mother Mary, Mary, mother of James, Salome, Luke 24:10... all up early to tend to Jesus' body, but He was not there! Unimaginable scene! Even more unbelievable that you were met with two angels proclaiming: *He Is Risen!*, Luke 24: 1-7, and to have Jesus Himself reveal that He was no longer in the tomb! REJOICE! Matthew 28:9.

I, too, understand the feeling of utter loss. On December 4, 1988, my brother John was taken by the Pacific Ocean in Oregon. We never got to see him again, but one day we shall. I can imagine the wonder as you walked on with the 11 those 40 days before Jesus' ascension until long after the Holy Spirit was promised and come Acts 2:1-4.

Thank you, Joanna and all your sisters of the Son, your strength, integrity, and undying love show me I should be doing so much more ... John 21:24-25. John, I can Only Imagine!!!

Mary Mother of Jesus

Alexia Harvey, *55 years old*

"Now the birth of Jesus Christ was as follows: After His mother Mary was betrothed to Joseph, before they came together, she was found with child of the Holy Spirit." Matthew 1:18

Mary, the mother of Jesus, found out that she was going to have a baby through an announcement by the angel Gabriel. Of course, when Mary heard this, she asked how that was possible, since she was a virgin, and Gabriel answered her in Luke 1: 35, *"The Holy Spirit will come upon you, and the power of the Highest will overshadow you; therefore, also, that Holy One who is to be born will be called the Son of God."* Now, Mary may not have fully understood the assignment at that time, but she answered in faith and trust. *"Let it be to me according to your word"* (Luke 1:38). She had no idea what the future would hold, but she had at least some knowledge of Scripture, and she knew this baby would be special. When Jesus was born, the shepherds who came to see Him and Mary and Joseph told them what the angels had said. *"For there is born to you this day in the city of David a Savior, which is Christ the Lord"* (Luke 2:11).

This special baby was the long-awaited Messiah. When Jesus was taken to the Temple to be presented to the Lord, Simeon declared that he could die now because he had seen the Christ. He then gave Mary a bit of foreshadowing of things to come. Luke 2:34-35 says, *"Then Simeon blessed them, and said to Mary His mother, 'Behold this Child is destined for the fall and rising of many in Israel, and for a sign which will be spoken against (yes, a sword will pierce through your own soul also), that the thoughts of many hearts may be revealed.'"* Scripture tells us that Mary remembered what was said of Jesus, and she pondered those things. As Jesus grew to be a young adult and was starting His ministry, I'm sure those words were never far from her mind. From Scripture, we know that she was around for His first miracle at the wedding at Cana. Can you just see her beaming with pride as the weddinggoers were served the wine He had just turned from water? Can you imagine her excitement to see His ministry grow and expand? She was a first-hand witness to the fulfilling of centuries of prophecy. And, when Jesus was arrested and tried, and an angry mob demanded His death, I feel certain that she was there, watching in absolute horror and heartbreak when her son was beaten until He was unrecognizable. As a mom, I cannot even imagine how hard that must have been for her to witness, and yet, I cannot imagine her walking away and leaving her son to suffer by Himself. Where else could she have been? When Jesus was crucified, we know Mary was there. And truly a sword must have pierced her soul. Her son, her firstborn, dying right there in front of her had to have shattered her heart. In the midst of all that sorrow, though, Mary had to trust God. She had to trust that He had a plan for Jesus, and He had a plan for her. What a paradox: hope and trust in the midst of abject heartbreak.

As a mom, I can relate to that paradox on a tiny scale of what Mary experienced. My son, Jonathan, was born full-term and healthy to a rather naïve, somewhat sheltered 27-year-old version of me. I had stars in my eyes about motherhood, and never considered that anything would happen to him. Interestingly, I had felt an overwhelming need to pray Psalm 91 over him. Daily. I read the whole chapter over him when he was in utero and for the first several months of his life, I felt strongly that verses 14-16 were what I needed to focus on when he was at his sickest. Those verses say, *"Because he has set his love upon Me, therefore I will deliver him; I will set him on high because he has known My name. He shall call upon me and I will answer him; I will be with him in trouble; I will deliver him and honor him. With LONG LIFE (my emphasis) I will satisfy him and show him my salvation."*

The day I realized that something was horribly wrong, Jonathan was just over four months old. He had begun grunting every time he took a breath. He was spitting up a lot, although he wasn't drinking much, and he had stopped having wet diapers. But the most alarming thing I noticed was that his soft spot was puffy. When I noticed that, I didn't wait for the pediatrician's office to call me back. I just drove Jonathan there. When the doctor came in and said she'd called an ambulance, I refused. I said, "No! Why would you call an ambulance?" The doctor replied that I didn't have a choice, the ambulance was coming, and Jonathan was a very sick little baby. Several hours later, a Pediatric Cardiologist came to talk with me, and told me that Jonathan was in Congestive Heart Failure. "Congestive Heart Failure?" I repeated. "That's an old person's disease." But the doctor assured me I was wrong. Anyone can have CHF, including my infant son. The next five months of life were a blur of doctor visits and hospital stays, capped off at the end with a heart transplant (his first).

It was in the days before his transplant that I began to think about Mary, the mother of Jesus. I was in Jonathan's hospital room, praying for him, praying over him, and asking God for a miracle. I knew that was what it would take for Jonathan. He had been in Pediatric ICU for nearly a month and had been on a ventilator the entire time. He was getting medicine to help his heart pump better, to raise his blood pressure, and to keep him still and quiet because he got so agitated when he was awake. I had seen doctors and nurses do unspeakable things to him, in the name of trying to save his life. I was heartbroken that doctors did not give him much chance for survival. Every time they came in to do something painful to him, in an effort to save his life, it pierced my very soul. I felt every pain like a sword through my heart. Yet, at the same time, I had hope that God would see us both through whatever the future held. And I trusted that God's plan for us was good. In the midst of utter heartbreak, I had hope and trust. His plan was good, and Jonathan thrived.

When Mary found out that she was going to be the mother of the Messiah, she was aware that her role was going to be a difficult one. And she had a front row seat to Jesus' life, which was also difficult. God never promises us that we won't have hardships. He just promises that He will be with us through them all. I knew that Jonathan's life, and my life as his mom, would not be easy. But I also knew, and I still know that God will see us through every difficulty in life. Psalm 23:4 says,

"Yea, though I walk through the valley of the shadow of death, I will fear no evil; for You are with me; Your rod and Your staff, they comfort me."

Sometimes, the outcome is not what we hope it will be, but God sees us through those times as well. I did not want Jonathan to have a heart transplant. I wanted him to be healed, and not have to endure all the pain and the lifelong medical issues that went along with a transplant, but God had a different plan. And His plan has been better than we could have ever dreamed or imagined. But we have had to live in that paradox of heartbreak and hope and trust on more than one occasion. When Jonathan was fifteen, he went into cardiac arrest at school. That whole day was a mix of heartbreak and hope. I was hopeful that it was a one-time thing. A fluke that doctors would get to the bottom of, then fix. But that was not the case. Jonathan's first transplant had gone bad. Catastrophically bad. Jonathan was revived but went into cardiac arrest again the next day at the hospital. A month later, he received another heart transplant. Another miracle. More heartbreak, watching him go through unspeakable pain. And again, I thought of Mary. How she watched Jesus suffer and die, and still she trusted God and she had hope. And hope did not disappoint. Mary saw her son whole and well again and rejoiced at God's promise fulfilled. My son is whole and well, and I rejoice at God's promise fulfilled.

If you find yourself in the midst of great sorrow or heartache, know that you are not alone. Your Heavenly Father is with you. His Word is full of verses that offer comfort; words of faith that will give you hope, and help you trust God's plan for your life. Hide those words in your heart and ponder them, dear sister. You have a great example of strength in Mary, the mother of Jesus. She endured such great heartbreak, yet she had hope that what Jesus said would come to pass. And she trusted God with the plan. You may not see how God is going to work out your situation, but trust Him, anyway. And remember, sometimes, the way He works things out isn't how we think they should be, but He is still God, and He is trustworthy. One of my favorite hymns says, "Heart of my own heart, whatever befall; still be my vision, Oh Ruler of all." No matter what, we trust Him. Just like Mary did. Her life was full of opportunities to question God and to lose hope. But she remained steadfast. She trusted God and she believed in her son, Jesus. Let her life be an encouragement to you to trust God and never lose hope, even when your heart is breaking.

Gabriel reminded Mary that, *"with God, nothing will be impossible"* Luke 1:37.

Dwell in possibility!

Miriam

Fely Woods, *46 years old*

"And when the cloud departed from above the tabernacle,
suddenly Miriam became leprous, as white as snow. Then Aaron turned
toward Miriam, and there she was, a leper."
Numbers 12:10

I was happy remembering Miriam as the rejoicing woman whose song of triumph is recorded in Exodus 15:20-21 right after Moses' song of praise to God for supernaturally bringing His people safely across the Red Sea. Her song is short and sweet, and her leading of the women in singing and dancing is beautiful! But later in her life, after such a beautiful start to her story, I see a turn down the same path I almost took which nearly trapped and enslaved me. It was by far the most intimidating demonic spirit I had ever faced, and the only one I didn't recognize until it was threatening to suffocate all the Lord had worked in my family over the previous two decades. I can't describe how camouflaged it was. But praise God, we heard His voice lead us out. I was called a witch and my husband was called a demon when we left. But the farther we got from that spirit, the sillier and weaker all of it became and the stronger we got in the Lord.

With Miriam, she was initially the deliverer of "the deliverer" in Exodus 2, rescuing three month old Moses from complete disconnection from his family. Moses was able to bond with his mother, learn from his father, and grow with his siblings (Aaron was three at the time) because of Miriam's intervention. So, Miriam starts off as a symbol of hope, a protector of what's good, a witness to the miraculous provision of God, and a catalyst to His purpose. As time went on, Miriam continued watching her brother from a distance, from the housing community for Hebrew slaves, as he grew up in wealth and luxury at the royal palace of the most powerful civilization in the world at that time. She likely knew when, as a grown man, he ended up murdering someone then running away in fear, not to be seen for forty long years. Though her life as a Hebrew remained in the same state of slavery and oppression through all of this, she then watched him return, in partnership with their brother Aaron, boldly declaring to be the spokesman of God for all Hebrew people. She watched God confirm His power through Moses before the hard-hearted Egyptian Pharaoh until Moses finally did obtain freedom for all the Hebrew people. Miriam saw every unique miracle God did as her brother led their people to freedom, and she led people in that triumphant worship song I mentioned before after they all crossed the sea on dry land.

She then built an established and solid history of walking with God in the proper position of leadership and with no mention of jealousy, division, or striving. She was married to Hur, according to Josephus in the Antiquities of the Jews, who is also identified as a close, trusted friend to Moses in Exodus 17:10 and 24:14, so both she and her husband were definite leaders in the whole nation of Israel. So then what happened? How did we get to Numbers 12:9-10 where God's anger rose against her, His presence left, and she became a leper? What could possibly have triggered a process in her heart that ended in her being publicly punished by God? Pride is a beast, and it activates a religious spirit that wraps tight around your faith to control it. And when it manifests through spiritual leaders, it rips through congregations in the sneakiest, most divisive, and destructive way! In Miriam's case, it was triggered by racism against Moses' choice of wife, and selfish ambition expressed in jealousy of Moses' recognition as the most powerful influencer of the people (read through Numbers 12:1-15) which are obvious sins. But in the personal situation where I faced the spirit of religion, the trigger was something good! It was triggered by a hunger for revival.

Have your Bibles out! I'll be giving lots of scriptures you'll want to read through... we had found a local fellowship (we'll call it Club X) that seemed so fun, fiery, and radically hard-core! They aggressively shouted for revival and praised zealously. They cried out in travailing prayer with such emotion! Our family was all in, sold out, and hungry as ever for a real revival to start like the ones we've always prayed for but only read about! But soon, we discerned something strange forming in the culture. The heart of false religion was growing in Club X leaders, manifesting in manipulative control, prideful elitism, and fear-based leadership. Now, looking back, I can clearly recognize the symptoms of it in Miriam's story. I will lay it all out for you, so you will never allow it to reach the levels of drama and disappointment that we naively allowed!

First, the spirit of religion fixates on taking control from the "top" to the "bottom," never understanding Jesus' words in Matthew 20:25-28. At Club X, the shouting from onstage ceased being a pure-hearted attempt to spark revival and shifted into angry shouting at the people to get louder and dance wilder "or else you're a threat to revival". We were continually warned that any disobedience to the leaders was rebellion and witchcraft, and they preached from the stage that "if you're a member here, then what we say is the literal Word of God for your family!" which is bold religious manipulation. We hung on, making excuses for their narcissism, but the spirit of religion was establishing its grip and the psychological chains it used were so oppressive! We eventually watched many families become so busy following the ever-growing number of detailed orders from that spirit of religion that they couldn't hear the voice of wisdom, so addictions and repetitive cycles of bondage were not being broken off and prevented, but just kept cycling through the people. Intercessors were put on stage with instructions to be loud, aggressive, and in precise alignment with specific religious mandates. You were considered the "elite" team of intercessors if you could perform on demand and pray loud for an extended time (Matthew 6:5-8 teaches otherwise!). Families were continually called to sacrifice everything on the altar of revival to "prove themselves worthy of carrying revival". That works-mentality exposes all you need to know about a culture (Romans 3:19-31 is key!).

In Miriam's story, she also wanted control over the people, as evidenced in Numbers 12:2, NRSV which says, *"and they said, 'Has the LORD spoken only through Moses? Has he not spoken through us also?' And the LORD heard it."* Religion is never satisfied! She was an eye-witness to every miraculous event that happened as God brought His people out of Egypt (see Micah 6:4) and her husband was honored to uphold the arms of Moses when he prayed on the hilltop in Exodus 17:10-13, but still she needed more recognition and power.

At Club X, some became so in love with their own voices that they would engage demons in long dialogues, asking their names, points of entrance, commanding officers names, favorite books, and preference in pizza toppings (just joking on the last two) and all loudly or on camera for everyone else to watch their performance. The religious spirit basically gave license to demons to put on a show and make a public spectacle at the expense of the poor person needing deliverance, all to feed carnal pride in appearing spiritually authoritative. I imagine it could've been similar with the Israelites had Miriam ended up prevailing in her fight for top position, and I can imagine this because of her failure to step up in faithfulness to God at the base of Mt. Sinai in Exodus 32. While the Bible doesn't specifically say so, where do you think Miriam was and what compromises might she have been making when all the people were dancing, singing, and praising their golden calf? As a leader of the women, where was she when this demonic show needed to be stopped? As a worship leader, did she help lead them in idol worship?

We can assume as well that Miriam actually led the religious discussion in those verses because she is mentioned before Aaron (and it's interesting that her punishment for criticizing the skin color of Moses' wife was for her own skin to turn white with disease). I believe that, as with most elitists, haughtiness and superiority was actually a means to cover insecurity about her position. But God answered by calling her front and center for a corrective conversation elevating His desired leader (who was the most humble man on the planet according to Numbers 12:3) and pointing out her pride in verses 6-10a.

Finally, about the "travailing" at Club X. We learned that religion can be very loud and appear devout, but will always lack the raw dunamis power needed for true healing, revival, restoration, and reformation! The religious spirit had people bound in travail that lacked faith to actually receive, because if they did, then what works would they have to perform anymore? Healings were occasional when guest speakers came but in normal services, it seemed loyalist emotion took over, yet real healing was stifled due to the spirit of religion in operation. Religion keeps people bound in a slavery mentality so they cannot fully identify as real sons of God, which rightly implies that they are made free (John 8:36). Satan loves this strategy of religion because it is fear-based, exactly like child-abusers and wife-beaters use; it's also a gang mentality. It breeds insecurity so that people will subconsciously continue striving for acceptance and worth, to maintain not just control, but a twisted form of loyalty. Victims have a need to perform, earn, make things happen, and even show off their tenacity, grit, or other characteristics they value. It yokes people like oxen and glorifies being heavily burdened by some noble cause. Read Matthew 11:28-30.

What started as a story of a young, brave girl who rescued her baby brother ended in an envious lust for control that caused the Lord Himself to defend that brother from her! And what started as a pure cry for revival in Club X was changed by the spirit of religion into what I recognize now as "Christian witchcraft," a term for what we see in Lucifer, the first worship leader, who pridefully stirred up a revolt for control long ago. Thankfully, just as our family was healed when we left the religious covering of that controlling spirit, Miriam was restored as Moses prayed and she realigned herself in proper order. She wasn't abandoned, rejected for her rebellion, or utterly demolished by His wrath like Korah's followers when they rebelled just a few chapters later in Numbers 16. But truth be told, after succumbing to the religious spirit and being punished, she disappeared from the Bible narrative until her death in Numbers 20:1, and in Deuteronomy 24:8-9 she is used as a warning and example of what not to do.

May we NEVER succumb to the religious spirit and forfeit our destiny! May you accept no spirit but the Holy Spirit in your families! And may the joy of the Lord and freedom in His presence mark you forever as His beloved son and daughter! In Jesus' name… amen.

Asenath

DeAnna L. Carl, *58 years old*

"And to Joseph in the land of Egypt were born Manasseh and Ephraim, whom Asenath, the daughter of Poti-Pherah priest of On, bore to him."
Genesis 46:20

ave you ever been put into a position in your life where your namesake was the ruling factor of your life's plan? Have you ever sacrificed beliefs/ingrained culture for love? How far are you willing to go to receive and accept God's plan for your life? Are you willing to cross cultural lines for God's will to be done? Let us revisit a time when an Egyptian woman of elite status, through her namesake, committed herself to a slave. With her husband, Joseph, she becomes a servant for life to the God of Israel. Moreover, her experience of motherhood produced an heir for the God of her new culture and not that of her Egyptian heritage. How deep can we go to understand how the God of our salvation intervenes cross culturally? Let us come with an open heart to understand the story of how a born Egyptian daughter came to be known world-wide as a Jewish monarch for God's purposes. In addition, I will share my own story of God's intervention in my cross-culture marriage.

An Egyptian Woman Whose Name Has a Purpose

Asenath was a high aristocratic Egyptian woman whose name meant "She belongs to her father". The namesake alone could pique the interest of any modern-day social tabloid. During Asenath's day, upper class Egyptian women normally obtained their positions based on their relationship with the men in their life. However, in the days of Asenath, wife of Joseph the dreamer, nothing could be more of an opportunity for societal fodder than an aristocrat's outlandish decision to marry one of lesser economic status. History and modern times reveal the overwhelming way in which people become preoccupied with the lives of the rich and famous. It is even more exciting when the two lovebirds are prominent figures in society. This provides more opportunity for society to weigh in on the life of the couple and whether or not they will make it. It is not unusual for outsiders to take it one step further and wager bets on the abnormal circumstances.

Daughter of the Priest

The society in which Asenath was born was of patriarchal dominance. In other words, back then, prominent societies lived up to the Godfather of Soul's most famous song; "This Is a Man's World." Those days and times in Egypt's history proved to be a man's world of dominance for both elite and lower-class women. Especially when the father/Pharoah all but presses Asenath to marry outside of her cultural lineage. Of course, we know that this strategy hardly works in this modern day. The pattern of male dominance continued in the life of a lower class, peasant Egyptian woman who normally worked alongside her man, or by herself if the man was away. In the lower classes, in the male's absence, the women were assigned various duties and ran the husband's businesses while he was away. Fortunately for Asenath, this was not her lifestyle. While they may have been publicly and socially viewed as inferior to men, Egyptian women enjoyed a great deal of legal and financial independence. Women could buy and sell property, serve on juries, make wills, and even enter into legal contracts. Egyptian women typically worked outside the home, but those who did usually received equal pay for doing the same jobs as men. In ancient Egypt, a woman enjoyed the same rights as a man. Her rights were dependent upon her social class and not her sex. Although Greek women lived in Egypt, they were not granted the same privileges as Egyptian women. They were supervised by a male guardian known as a Kyrios.

Historically many of the women never knew their rights like women of today. Therefore, they never exercised their rights. There were no hindrances for total equality within the Egyptian culture as far as women were concerned. Unlike the women of ancient Greece, who effectively were owned by the husbands, Egyptian women also had the right to divorce and remarry. Egyptian couples were even known to negotiate prenuptial agreements. We currently see this in modern day culture where women are initiating prenuptials just as much as men. Another task women could freely perform was contract negotiations that listed all the property and wealth the woman had brought into the marriage and guaranteed compensation in the event of a divorce. However, one central control of Egyptian lifestyle was that of peace and harmony. In order to have peace and harmony in society, one of the primary duties of the Pharaoh in the elite circles was to orchestrate the marriages for the greater good of financial and possible military dominance. The namesake of Asenath holds true to the manifesting of the leading of her father and Pharoah in marrying Joseph, the dreamer. Additionally, in the Word of God, it is revealed how the meaning of her name was manifested for all of society to see.

In Genesis 41:45, it is written that the father Asenath belonged to gave her away into a cross cultural union. Ancient elite societies subjected themselves to cross culture relationships for their advantages. Asenath was given to her husband seemingly without her input. Normalized by the Egyptian culture, Asenath was given away by the one who reared and covered her. One could wonder what the course of strategy was used by the wise and eternal God to keep the heart of her father and Pharaoh from promising her to another. How did the Lord restrain her father from promising her to another? Asenath was the daughter of Potiphera, the priest of On, who served under Pharaoh Sesostris II. What is most fascinating is how Asenath's namesake connects to what happens during the course of her life. Genesis 41:45 states, *"And Pharaoh called Joseph's name Zaphenath-Paneah. And he gave him in marriage, Asenath, the daughter of Potiphera Priest of On. So, Joseph went out over the land of Egypt."* Asenath was devoted to worship of her gods. Although a worshipper of pagan deities, it was necessary that she convert to Judaism. Through God directed matters, Asenath becomes the suitable wife for Joseph, the dreamer. Pharaoh could not offer to Joseph any woman not even of his own lineage but a daughter of the priesthood of the true God. Genesis 24:51 states,

"Behold, Rebekah is before you; take her and go, and let her be the wife of your master's son, as the Lord has spoken."

Wife of A Hebrew Slave

Asenath became the wife of a Hebrew slave named Joseph, the dreamer, son of Jacob. Joseph was betrayed by his brothers, sold into slavery by them, and then his coat of many colors was dipped in blood and used to cover the wrong his brothers had done to him. Though imprisoned, he became known as a dream interpreter for Yahweh. Joseph was elevated to power by Pharaoh Sesostris II after he experienced firsthand that Joseph was chosen by The God of Israel. Joseph rose to power in Egypt and became second in command. Then, the Lord God used Joseph as a tool to transfer wealth from His own people. Acts 7:10 says, *"...and rescued him from all his troubles. He granted Joseph favor and wisdom in the sight of Pharoah, king of Egypt, who appointed him ruler over Egypt and all his household."* Genesis 37-50 states, *"This proposal pleased Pharaoh and all his servants and Pharaoh said to his servants, 'Can we find a man like this, in whom is the spirit of God?'"* By interpreting dreams for Pharoah, Joseph was rewarded an Egyptian wife from a high-profile family. Of all the stories in the Bible of people's lives being parallel, this is certainly one to note. Joseph was a slave who married a woman of elite status and Joseph, in turn, was elevated from enslavement to elite status. In the Word of God, there is nothing negative written about Joseph marrying Asenath.

Mother of Sons Who Birthed Forefathers of the 12 Tribes of Israel

Does someone of foreign faith belong in the bloodline of not one, but two, Israelite tribes? Asenath was the mother of Manasseh and Ephraim who became forefathers to two of the 12 tribes of Israel.

Genesis 46:20 says, *"Manasseh and Ephraim were born to Joseph in the land of Egypt by Asenath daughter of Potiphera, Priest of On."*

Genesis 48:5 states, *"And now your two sons born to you in Egypt before I came to you here shall be reckoned as mine; Ephraim and Manasseh shall be mine, just as Rueben and Simeon are mine."* Genesis 41:50-52 says, *"Before the years of famine arrived, two sons were born to Joseph by Asenath, daughter of Potiphera, Priest of On. Joseph named the firstborn Manasseh, saying, "God has made me forget all my hardship and all my father's household. And the second son he named,*

Ephraim, saying, "God has made me fruitful in the land of my afflic-tions" Genesis 48:14. states, *"But Israel stretched out his right hand and put it on the head of Ephraim, the younger; and crossed his hands, he put his left on Manasseh's head, although Manasseh was the first born."* Joshua 14:4 says, *"The descendants of Joseph became two tribes, Manasseh and Ephraim. And no portion of the land was given to the Levites, except for cities in which to live, along with pasturelands for their flocks and herds."*

In today's society, people are no longer making decisions based on previous cultural standards which dictated how marriages were arranged. Fortunately, I was in a position where I could choose, in alignment with God's will, who I would marry. For over twenty years, I have been in a cross culture relationship. In this modern time, people do not take notice of cross cultural relationships unless the family name is tied to wealth. Neither myself nor my husband were born aristocrats nor had to give up our heritage. But we merged the beliefs and customs of our cultures to align ourselves with God's will.

In the same way Joseph had to become accustomed to the Egyptian culture, my husband had to become accustomed to the African American culture. This was an easy transition for my husband because in learning about the culture, he learned more about me. My husband grew up with only one African American person in the entire high school he attended. His first time seeing an African American was in junior high school. However, his cultural learning curve was easy and successful because of his acceptance and love of my culture. This is similar to how Joseph was able to embrace the Egyptian culture.

Conversely, the similarities between me and Asenath are close. Just as she resisted Joseph, I resisted my husband's advances because of my own ideologies of who I should marry. But as it was proven over time, the trajectory of Asenath's life, marriage, and the future of Israel was preplanned by the Most High God. After a year of pursuing me, God revealed His will was operating all along and at that point, culture no longer mattered. As with Joseph and Asenath, after one encounter, my husband and I realized culture no longer mattered. Regardless of who speaks unfavorably against your relationship or does not support it, God has the final say.

Bathsheba

Susan R. McCormick, *54 years old*

"The man said, "She is Bathsheba, the daughter of Eliam and the wife of Uriah the Hittite." 2 Samuel 11:3

In one of the most dramatic accounts in the Old Testament is the story of Bathsheba, who was a beautiful woman that was tangled up in a life of adultery, murder, grief, and chaos. She is said to have been a wise, protective, counselor to her son Solomon, Queen Mother (the most powerful position a woman could hold) in Israel, and loyal wife of King David. Her story is one of sadness, betrayal, loyalty, and faithfulness. Her story begins in 2 Samuel 11:1-3, *"In the spring, at the time when kings go off to war, David sent Joab out with the king's men and the whole Israelite army. They destroyed the Ammonites and besieged Rabbah. But David remained in Jerusalem. One evening David got up from his bed and walked around on the roof of the palace. From the roof he saw a woman bathing. The woman was very beautiful, and David sent someone to find out about her. The man said, "She is Bathsheba, the daughter of Eliam and the wife of Uriah the Hittite"* NIV.

King David was captivated by Bathsheba's beauty when he looked upon her as she was bathing. He should have been on the battlefield with his army that night. Kings were anointed for battle; David was anointed for battle. When kings are not in position, they are subject to the attacks of the enemy. David failed God that evening and several to follow. Yet, God called him a man after His own heart because he always turned and repented of his sins. Many times in Scripture, it is signified that priests and kings were only anointed while wearing their garments (robes); once the garments were removed, the anointing was gone! When we take our eyes off the Lord and place them onto other things and people, we, too, are subject to the enemy's attacks. Oh, but for the grace of God, the precious anointing of God could not touch the unclean flesh of man, all were unclean until the shedding of Jesus' precious blood on Calvary's tree. Now, we can carry that anointing within us to break sin's hold, every yoke, at all times! Hallelujah! Be sure our sins will carry consequences that can seemingly go beyond what you are able to bear. 2 Samuel 24:1-24, reveals to us that the Prophet Nathan was sent to expose King David's sins of adultery and murder. David had not only taken Bathsheba in a moment of heated passion but also had her husband sent to the frontlines to be killed. Because of this, the Lord required the firstborn of Bathsheba and David. It was not until David repented that God gave them another son, Solomon who would become heir to the throne and eventually King.

King Solomon was dearly loved by God, so much so, that the Prophet Nathan called him, *Jedidiah*, meaning *"beloved of Jehovah"*. One can only imagine the heartache Bathsheba faced losing her husband to death and then her first-born son, in a palace filled with so much sin and chaos. In it all, she stood faithful as a loving wife to King David and a wonderful mother to Solomon. God will bring good out of the ashes of sin, in the worse possible situations. He will redeem! I, too, am a living testimony to Christ's redeeming power having been raised the daughter of a Pentecostal preacher, knowing and receiving Christ at a young age and then turning my back on all that I believed in. I walked straight into hell. I was at the innocent age of twelve when we moved to Houston, Texas. Daddy was pastoring a good-sized church there, with our living quarters next door. It was in that parsonage that I remember lying awake at night trying to say some of the terrible words I had heard at school, since moving to Houston. I was the new kid, I wanted to *just* fit in. I would say a "bad" word in my head, I couldn't even get it out of my mouth. Then, I would think, "Oh, that sounds horrible, I can't do this."

Until one day at school, I began to speak them out loud to my "friends". I became a professional at cussing and had been sent by Houston's finest to a juvenile detention center. This began many "bad" habits and terrible choices in my life. Bringing shame and dishonor to my God-fearing "pastor" parents was probably the heaviest of the guilt I carried, well into adulthood. James 1:5 states, *"Then when lust hath conceived, it bringeth forth sin: and sin, when it is finished, bringeth forth death."*

My mother used to tell us, "Sin will take you further than you want to go, make you stay longer than you want to stay, and make you pay more than you want to pay." Oh, how true this is. I dropped out of school and by the age of sixteen, I was married and pregnant with my first-born son. I did not wait for God to bring me the man He alone had prepared for me. I was anxious to get this life started. A little girl's fantasy soon became a grown woman's nightmare. After eight years of marriage and three children, my world was shattered by learning that the same wonderful husband, whom I dearly loved, had been committing adultery and child molestation of several young girls in the church we attended. I was trying to lead these same young girls to Jesus, the best I could at my age, when my world and everything in it collapsed. Time stood still. My mother called one night to tell me of having a vision, it was of me running as fast as I could and shattering in a million pieces when I hit a brick wall. I felt it. I knew emotionally I could not ever begin to pick up all the shattered pieces of my broken life, alone. I wish I could tell you that in that moment I turned to God for strength and guidance. But my faith was not yet there. I didn't. I turned away from God even the more. At the age of twenty-one years, I was divorced and terrified. I carried the wages of sin into several marriages, all ending in devastating divorce. But it was not until the passing of my precious mother in November of 2005, that I fell completely apart. Once again, I faced the worst possible situation I could think of when God called her home. My mother was my confidant, my best friend, and my prayer warrior. So, I blamed God. In a moment of unanswered questions, I yelled at God, "How dare you take the only person that believed in me, the only person that ever loved me!" "How could You do this to ME?" "You must not love me!" Just those words coming out of my mouth led me into years of believing God did not love me (the loneliest I had ever felt). I began to frequent the local bars. I became an alcoholic for over two years, drinking from the time I woke up until the time I passed back out.

I went on to marry an alcoholic. Eleven years of my life with a man I loved, whom was my best friend when sober and my worst enemy when drunk. I never knew who I was going home to. I finally moved out, we lived five years apart and remained married. I could not bear to lose my best friend but could not live anymore with my worst enemy. My life was at stake, both spiritually and physically. God provided an open door for me to leave. It was in this house that I truly learned of God's redeeming love. I normally prayed and spent time with the Lord on my way to work, in my car, this day, however, I was not going to be in my car. Feeling somewhat frustrated, I asked the Lord, *"Where can I go just to be alone with you?"* The Lord directed me to my closet, I began a long journey in that closet. For the next 365, minus 1 day, I was on my knees, in my closet, on purpose, praying and building a relationship with my Father. Most importantly, I grew to not only know Jesus more and personally, but I fell in love with Jesus. My mother used to tell me, *"The difference will come when you fall in love with Jesus,"* and those words have never rang truer than they do today! I was not sure how to *fall in love* with Jesus. I had mastered loving a man I could see, I just wasn't sure how to love one I couldn't see, but her words echoed in my ear. I, on my knees in my dark closet one night asked the Lord, "Will you teach me how to love You, I want to Lord, I just don't know how, not like momma talks about?" Day after day, I learned to fall in love with Jesus. Today, He alone is my heart's desire.

One day, I was blow drying my hair and I kept feeling a pull into my closet (I had spent enough time with the Lord that I knew when He wanted to speak to me); finally, I just stopped drying my hair and went into my closet. I knelt and said, "What is it, Lord?" He said, *"My people, they don't love me."* I said, "Lord, how can they be your people and not love you?" He said, *"Because their hearts are far from me!"* My heart broke right there, I cried for a while and begin to pray, all of a sudden, the Lord said, *"I just wanted to say thank you for loving me."* I do not say this to brag, I say it to encourage you to fall in love with Jesus, He desires for you to love Him. There is nothing He desires more than you to love Him, even all your works, nothing means more to Him than your heart, all of it! It was in my closet where I taught my grandson how to pray. My grandson was touched by this so much so, when others would come to the house, he would grab them by the hand and say, "Come on, we have to go pray," and he would lead them to my closet and proclaim that **Jesus lives in grandma's closet**. I am reminded of the scripture, *"Train up a child in the way he should go, And when he is old he will not depart from it"* Proverbs 22:6.

When I started the journey of seeking God, I never realized what I would go through. The Lord first showed me things He was not pleased with and I began repenting, getting those things out of my life, mind, and heart. One of the biggest things I faced was unforgiveness, as you can imagine. When we do not forgive, God cannot forgive us; knowing this, I knew I had to search the deep places and find out what all and who all I needed to forgive. There were things I had buried so deep that I did not remember until the Lord brought it to my attention, that I dealt with it. Forgiveness is never an easy task, but if you allow God to show you, you can repent and truly forgive, making way for liberty and forgiveness. I have gotten good at not allowing unforgiveness to creep in by forgiving quickly, I do it on purpose. Much of what we face in this life requires us to forgive an act, forgive someone else, and to forgive ourselves. Read Matthew 6:14. It was in that closet that I felt it was time to be ordained into ministry on January 10th, 2016. I knew I was called from a young child to preach the Gospel of Jesus Christ. Today, I am a Pastor and founder of Joplin Street Revival. Read Jeremiah 29:11.

He knows the plans He has for you, there is a book about you, yes, you, in Heaven. Ask and He will reveal what His plans are for your life, and that journey will begin when you fall on your knees in prayer and in love with Jesus. My first message, at my ordination service, was taken from 2 Chronicles 7:14, *"If my people, which are called by my name, shall humble themselves, and pray, and seek my face, and turn from their wicked ways; then will I hear from heaven, and will forgive their sin, and will heal their land."* Oh, what redeeming love from my wonderful Savior. He will do the same for you! Bathsheba's story is full of God's redemptive power, love, mercy, and grace and I am sure just like me, she would agree, your flesh will die a million deaths in accomplishing the will of God. Yet, in every "God Purpose" battle there are glorious victories that follow, if you dare to kneel before the King of Kings.

Rizpah

Misty Mott, *46 years old*

"Rizpah, daughter of Aiah, took sackcloth and spread it out for herself on a rock. From the beginning of harvest till the rain poured down from the heavens on the bodies she did not let the birds of the air touch them by day or the wild animals by night." 2 Samuel 21:10

My husband was at work. The children had gone to school. The house was quiet; my heart was screaming. Once again, being a mother of two teenage boys in Gen Z had taken its toll on me. It had been a dark season with very little light. The waves of warfare were relentless. These two boys that God had entrusted to me, that I had been faithful to pray over since the day I knew I was pregnant, appeared to be drowning in the darkness of their culture. I turned out the lights. I locked all the doors. And on the living room floor that day, I laid before the Lord my broken heart and frail cry. And just as promised in Psalm 18:2, He came. *"I cried out to you in my distress, the delivering God, and from your temple-throne you heard my troubled cry. My sobs came right into your heart and you turned your face to rescue me."* Gently, but firmly, I heard Him say, "Rise up and be a Rizpah." And with those words, what I would soon discover is that on this day, He didn't just come for me; but for a generation.

Within the pages of 2 Samuel 21, you will find a devastated mother of two boys. She finds herself in a place no mother ever wishes to experience. Yet while staring at the corpses of her dead sons, she finds a strength that is nothing short of other worldly. Rizpah's two sons, Armoni and Mephibosheth, were brutally killed with their bodies left hanging exposed due to the sins of their father, Saul. It would probably be a good time to note that the compromise of one generation will always show up in the next. The verdict was the bodies would remain unburied until the heavens opened and the late heavy rains would come. Since their land had been in a famine for three years, this judgment seemed to carry an intense level of cruelty and brutality. Nevertheless, it did not stop this momma. With a bull dog determination, Rizpah decides she will not move until the rain comes. She takes a sackcloth (which symbolizes repentance, consecration, and intercession) and spreads it out on a rock. She takes her position right next to the gallows. She refuses to put herself at a distance from darkness, death, and the stench of sin.

Days. Weeks. Months. A Rizpah will stay in intercession until it rains. A Rizpah will stay in the fight until the giant goes down. For a Rizpah, there is no option to throw in the towel and go home. *"Ask, and the gift is yours. Seek, and you'll discover. Knock, and the door will be opened for you. For every persistent one will get what he asks for. Every persistent seeker will discover what he longs for. And everyone who knocks persistently will one day find an open door"* Matthew 7:7-8.

Rizpah was not able to prevent the exposure but she gave her life to prevent the devouring. She did not let the birds of the air touch them by day nor the wild animals by night. Rizpah could not stop the exposure of sin that came to her sons but she would give everything she had, day and night, to ward off the vultures from consuming them. Vultures can smell the chemical compounds of decaying flesh miles away. They will begin to circle around downward until they find the odor's origin. Then, they proceed to pick at the dead flesh until their corpses are completely unrecognizable. Gross, I know, but your enemy is no different. He will swarm around pockets of difficulties, weaknesses, and trauma in your children's lives. If left undealt with or fought against, he will pick at them until their identity and purpose is utterly consumed. This is why Rizpah's must arise in this hour! She will position herself between the vultures and the corpses of her sons. She will risk violence from the wild beast herself. A Rizpah will place themselves in between the enemy and their loved ones. There they will stay, they will weep, they will keep watch. Until.

Did you know the easiest way to keep a vulture away is to make loud noises? You must do this immediately at the sight of them, giving them no opportunity to settle, land, or lodge. The moment you see them, run out there and make all the racket you can while waving your arms, as you move towards the enemy. Psalm 149:5-9 says, *"Their joyful praises fill their mouths, for their shouted praises are their weapons of war! These warring weapons will bring vengeance (retaliation, repayment) on every opposing force and every resistant power – to bind kings with chains and rulers with iron shackles. Praise filled warriors will enforce the judgment-doom decreed against their enemies."* A Rizpah knows how to open their mouth. They will refuse to remain silent while demonic vultures ravish their children. A Rizpah will look death straight in the eye and decree the Word of the Lord over their child. A Rizpah will cut off the enemy's assignment with her shouts of praise. Her high praise will send a declaration to hell, "You can come this far and no more!"

Gen Z is anyone that was born between the years of 1997-2012, currently between the ages of 11-26. This is a generation like no other. The enemy absolutely hates this generation. He has targeted them even at birth with identity crisis, mental confusion, self-harm, anxiety, depression, perversion, sexual confusion, and bondage. They have been labeled by medical research as the most anxious and depressed generation to date. The enemy must be scared to death of them! He only releases warfare equal to a threat. Rizpahs Arise! Get in between death and this generation. Get in between hell and this generation! Get in between them and the destruction and prophesy their destiny! Refuse to move until there is Revival. Open your mouth and cry out! *"Open your mouth with a mighty decree; I will fulfill now, you'll see! The words you speak, so shall it be!"* Psalm 81:10.

On that day in the living room, I saw no natural way out. I felt I was at the end and there was no way to really go back. But what I thought was a dead end was actually a birthing. His faithfulness is mind boggling. He responded to my cry that day. He began the process of healing my heart and my family but He also opened my womb to a generation. He released a *Rizpah Roar* in my spirit for my own sons and an entire generation. I began to spend hours in intercession for all the "Rizpah sons". I began to shout, praise, and dance over them. He gave me His heart for this generation. He allowed me to see them the way He sees them. The Holy Spirit began to take me through travail, so the Father's destiny for this generation could break through. Now, with the help of my local church, we are hosting Regional Gen Z Rallies. We are seeing trauma healed, identities restored, and prisons emptied. This generation that was targeted by the enemy has been marked by God and they are arising as a mighty army in this hour. *"But Yahweh says:"The prey will be freed from the mighty warrior and captives will be rescued from a conqueror! For I will fight with those who fight with you, and I myself will save your children"* Isaiah 49:25.

Speak these declarations over your child or loved ones in Gen Z:

- I decree the devil is a liar.
- I decree the narrative of the enemy for their life is silenced and the narrative of God for their life is amplified.
- I stand up to the chaos and confusion in this generation and I command you to be silenced in Jesus' Name.
- Every trap and snare of the enemy be revealed and destroyed by the power of the Name of Jesus.
- Every assignment from hell be broken.
- I command every demon to loosen its grip on your mind.
- I command every unclean spirit to go.
- There is no bondage greater than God.
- Every bit of perversion, deception and addiction be consumed by the fire of God.
- I break every habitual cycle of sin and shame now in Jesus' Name.
- I take the keys that He has given me in Isaiah 22:22 and unlock the destiny, will, and purpose of God for your life, now!

RISE UP RIZPAH'S!

Naomi

Deana Thompson, *48 years old*

"And Naomi said to her two daughters-in-law, "Go, return each to her mother's house. The Lord deal kindly with you, as you have dealt with the dead and with me." Ruth 1:8

The Book of Ruth is a powerful book in the Bible. Most of us love the moving tale of the young brave woman Ruth, who endures tragic loss but finds love and redemption. However, have you considered that there may not have been a Book of Ruth without Naomi's influence in her life? Ruth begins with Naomi following her husband to another country to seek a better life due to famine. Despite their best intentions, she ends up as a widow and, years later, loses both of her sons. She was then left with her two daughters-in-law, Orpah and Ruth. She experienced great loss and suffering. Hearing that the famine had ended, Naomi decided to return to her homeland with her daughters-in-law, but soon changed her mind and encouraged them to return to their own relatives. Orpah went back to familiarity, while Ruth clung tightly to Naomi. In Hebrew, the word for "cling tightly" is *davqah*. This word implies a permanent bonding and signifies a covenantal devotion. What was it about Naomi that caused Ruth to cling to her? What blessings came upon Ruth because of her bond with Naomi? Ruth could have let logical thinking allow doubt to influence her decision and choose to leave Naomi. No one would have blamed her for returning home to her family and looking for a husband. In fact, it would have been expected. Instead, her heart came to grips with what she believed and desired, and she refused to let go of Naomi. Behind the scenes, God was at work.

It's important to note that Naomi still struggled. When she returned home with Ruth, she was clearly in a state of self-pity and bitterness. Her hometown was abuzz when she returned, but she told them to no longer call her Naomi but to call her Mara because the Lord had dealt bitterly with her. Naomi means sweet and pleasant, while Mara means bitterness. In her great loss and grief, she gave herself a new identity of bitterness. She continued to declare to them that the Lord had brought her home empty and afflicted. She lost hope for a future, thinking her family line had ended. Don't you love her raw honesty? She allowed others to see her real struggles. She had emotions, feelings, dreams, and desires. She let us peer into her soul and see the tension between suffering and faith. Nevertheless, God continued to work and move in her life. Naomi continued to pour into Ruth despite her own difficult time. She continued instructing and teaching Ruth about many things, including her homeland's customs. Naomi wisely counseled Ruth to go to Boaz's field to glean. After Ruth's encounter with Boaz, Naomi advises Ruth, saying, *"It is good, my daughter, that you go out with his young women, and that people do not meet you in any other field"* Ruth 2:22, NKJV. Naomi's heart stayed positioned for Ruth to succeed and find happiness. Despite her significant loss, she desired Ruth to find a home and a husband. Read Ruth 3:1-6.

Naomi taught Ruth how to go to Boaz in a humble and submissive way. Boaz found favor in Ruth and followed the appropriate customs to make her his wife. Naomi continued to wisely counsel Ruth to wait patiently. *"Then she said, "Sit still my daughter until you know how the manner will turn out; for the man will not rest until he has concluded the matter this day"* Ruth 3:18. Ruth was teachable and honored Naomi. Because Naomi opened her heart and life to Ruth, Ruth met her future husband, Boaz. She continued to be loving and show concern for Ruth and helped to pioneer the way for Ruth to be redeemed and restored. In Ruth 4, verses 10-12, Boaz obtains Ruth as his wife. The people who were at the gate and the elders declared that they were witnesses and spoke great blessings of prosperity over them. After that, the Bible states that Ruth and Boaz conceived and bore a son. Afterward, the women began to bless Naomi.

"Then the women said to Naomi, "Blessed be the Lord, who has not left you this day without a close relative; and may his name be famous in Israel! And may he be to you a restorer of life and a nourisher of your old age; for your daughter-in-law who loves you, who is better to you than seven sons, has borne him" Ruth 4:14-15.

"Also, the neighbor women gave him a name, saying, "There is a son born to Naomi," And they called his name Obed. He is the father of Jesse, the father of David" Ruth 4:17.

Naomi starts to come alive again, and hope begins to arise in her soul. Joy was restored to her. As Naomi helped Ruth succeed, Naomi's life was restored. She now had a secure future. God had turned her bitter into sweet, Mara back to Naomi. Out of Ruth and Boaz's lineage came the Messiah. That day, Naomi saw the goodness of God through generational legacy. Have you ever been in a place in your life where you experienced great loss and suffering? Where grief began to shift your identity, and you found yourself in a place of great bitterness? I have. But I've also seen God's goodness restore and redeem as I continued to minister to others and remain faithful. During Bible college, the Lord began to speak to my husband and I about church planting. We carried this dream in our hearts, trusting the Lord for the right time and place. After graduating, we worked in different places and in various capacities for a season. Several years after graduation, my husband was in an explosive accident that left him severely injured. He had to undergo skin grafts and suffered a broken back, which required two back surgeries and all the physical therapy that the recovery process entailed. This famine season of our life brought us to a pivotal moment. We felt like now was the time to relocate and start fresh. We moved to another state and became successful business owners. We were financially prosperous and flourishing. During this time, we also initiated the church plant. We started humbly but fervently in a home with a handful of people. Very quickly, our body began to really grow. We began to rent a facility to accommodate the number of people attending. It was a beautiful time in which we felt that we had truly launched out from the familiar and found a better life.

Years later, through a series of events, we found ourselves losing our home, our business, and some close relationships. To top it off, it felt like our church was falling apart as well. It seemed like everything was crumbling around us. It felt like we were starting all over again. I felt that God gave us a prosperous life, and then God took it from us. I saw myself holding my life in my hands like sand and watching helplessly as every grain slid through my fingers. I felt embarrassed about our great loss and even began to blame myself for it. I felt helpless and hopeless for a time, but I knew God's heart enough to know He was a good Father, and He was faithful. So many things were stripped from us, but we allowed that to return us to Jesus as our first love. As difficult as that time was, I remained vulnerable and transparent to those faithful sons and daughters who clung to us. We NEVER forgot that someone was always watching. This was our time to practice what we preached. Amid our suffering and our losses, we remained faithful to God and chose to pour into those around us. Naomi was a bridge between Ruth and future generations. Even when it was all falling apart, I wanted to be a bridge to the Ruths in my life. I began asking myself, "What if this really isn't about me? What if this is about the generations to come after me?" Once this shift in my heart happened, I began to see God turn my wilderness into a garden. I opened my eyes and saw His goodness in every space of life. His sovereignty reigned, and I saw God's faithfulness to complete what He had started.

God has now restored all things greater than before. Our new reality is better than our dreams. The church plant is now a 15-year-old flourishing family of believers. Through a series of events that could have only been orchestrated by God Himself, our church purchased a building that was being used as a bar in the nearby city of Mount Carmel, IL, that we have since renovated to become our beautiful church home. Sometime after our body moved to Mount Carmel, we did some digging into the history of the city. To our wonder and amazement, we found that the name Mount Carmel means "God's garden!" We are experiencing revival in our church; the addicts are being saved, and the lame are being healed. The broken-hearted are finding joy, and genera-tions are returning to the Father. Now, God has given us a beautiful home, and we are walking in His provision daily. Most importantly, my Ruths are flourishing. I'm beginning to see my biological and spiritual grandchildren worshipping and serving Jesus. I live in a state of awe and wonder at the Lord's redemption in my life.

Everyone has experienced great loss and suffering. That may look different from person to person, but the simple truth remains the same: suffering is suffering, and pain is pain. Our grief is real, and our pain cannot be invalidated simply because it is not the same as another's. Remember, though, we can still help others while going through our own difficulties. God has a plan in the middle of our pain. Sometimes, God might take us to places we do not understand, and we may walk through a season that we would have never chosen for ourselves. What if this is because He is preparing someone else for their destiny through learning from our experiences? What if the next generation reaps what we are sowing right now? Could the process you go through in your deep pain be the very thing that gets someone else into their purpose? The story of Naomi and Ruth is a powerful reminder that God always has a plan for our lives and works all things out for our good. No matter how impossible your situation may look in the moment, God is faithful to complete what He started. Romans 8:28 says, *"And we know that all good things work together for good to those who love God, to those who are the called according to His purpose."* God is always in control. It may take you by surprise, but it doesn't take Him by surprise. If Naomi's loss hadn't sent her back to her homeland, Ruth would never have met Boaz. God knows the end from the beginning. If only Naomi could have seen in the beginning how greatly the Lord would bless her at the end.

I encourage you to remain faithful to the Father and to watch and see what He can do. Don't question God's goodness in your life. May you be awakened to just how big God is and marvel at His goodness continually. If you are walking through a season of your life that is full of suffering and pain, remember the Ruths in your life. Who are you connected to? What are you connected to? Take a look around you, pour into the people around you, and trust God in the unknown. You have no idea who is at the other end of your obedience. He is the author and finisher of our faith. As you gaze on Him, you'll find your eyes get filled with light, and you can clearly see your wilderness turn into a garden.

Leah

Tammy Long Holloway, *60 years old*

"Now Laban had two daughters: the name of the elder was Leah, and the name of the younger was Rachel." Genesis 29:16

From Rejection to Rejoicing

Genesis Chapter 29 gives us a glimpse into the life of Leah. However, the subtitle of the chapter, as listed in the King James Version of the Bible is "Jacob Comes to the Well of Haran". It tells of the story of how Jacob meets and is smitten by the beauty of Rachel. It speaks of how Jacob was willing to work seven years in order to marry Rachel. His committed love for Rachel was celebrated and finally the marriage day had arrived. The marriage feast takes place and now Jacob goes into the tent to consummate his long-awaited love. Jacob makes passionate love during the night to who he assumed was Rachel; but when he awakens in the morning, to his dismay, he see Leah. Jacob exclaims to Laban according to Genesis 29:25 (NKJV) "What is *this* you have done to me? … and this is where Leah's journey with Jacob begins… Or does it? Leah is described in the scripture, depending on the version, as having weak eyes, lovely eyes, dull eyes, and attractive eyes; and in comparison; Rachel is described, in every version, as beautiful in form and appearance. In other words, people viewed Rachel as beautiful and there was nothing special about Leah. I imagine these sentiments were prevalent throughout their childhood.

I can relate to Leah's story. See, my story began with being born to a teenage mother; a girl who was looked down upon because she was seduced by a handsome, more experienced young man. He took advantage of her innocence. She had relations with him once (which no one believed; but I later confirmed it was true) and once he had conquered, he left her to deal with the shame and guilt. Therefore, as I was being raised at an early age, I felt guilt and shame too; it wasn't intentional but now, I know it was the enemy. He starts early trying to pervert and thwart the destiny that God has predestined for us before we were in our mother's womb, regardless of how we got there. My mother went on to meet a man that I called my stepdad. He was the father of all of my siblings. I was the only one without a dad. I respected this man because he was good to my mom, as good as he knew how to be; you see, at the time, neither he nor my mom knew the Lord. So, anytime there was drinking, there was arguing and that was often; it was just the way we lived. But all in all, he was a good man. He worked, he provided for the family, and he never treated me badly, but he also never treated me like a daughter. He treated me like Mary's child. He never said that in my hearing, but I felt it. Somehow, I came to accept that as care. I remember when we would go to his mother's house, my sibling's grandmother, and in speaking to friends or neighbors who would ask if we were her grandchildren, she would reply "Yes, but that's (pointing to me) Mary's daughter." As an adult, a born-again adult, I came to appreciate being recognized as Mary Long's daughter. Not just because I looked like her but my mother had a beautiful spirit and genuinely cared about all people, as well.

However, growing up and feeling rejected by my father, my actions screamed for acceptance by always trying to be the best, and not hanging with the wrong crowd. I was saying, "SEE ME, WANT ME, VALIDATE ME. As I grew to middle school and high school, I wanted to prove him wrong. To make him regret not claiming me and win the validation from without that I couldn't get from within. So, I was determined to; compelled, to be better! To excel in school, in 4H Club, in track, honor society, cheerleading, writing, modeling, and dancing. Yes, I got recognition and accolades from those activities; but still, it didn't satisfy the longing that was deep inside. As we look at Leah, I can imagine how she felt. Leah knew she wasn't Jacob's first choice. But I believe that somewhere in her heart, she believed that once he had made love to her, he would feel differently. Can you imagine the hurt and rejection that she felt when she saw his reaction and heard the words "What is *this?*" Oh, how her heart must have hurt. He didn't even say "who is this" and yes, Jacob was talking about the deceit of Laban, but Leah... heard the man she had given her virginity and her heart to; not even mention what they shared that night... he was only concerned with Rachel. The spirit of rejection continues to embed its tentacles down within Leah. From a child she wasn't the "special" one with the outward beauty that everyone could see and admire. Now, that which was so precious and sacred; that which she saw as a once in a lifetime gift, was tossed aside like it meant nothing. This was Leah's life.

Like so many of us, we get used to a certain state and just accept it as simply our lot in life. But if you look close, Leah was still hopeful that a change was possible. Again, this is a reflection from when I was growing up and my attempts to prove to people that I was valuable and worthy of acceptance by excelling in academics, sports, and other extracurricular activities failed and was treated like it was nothing special. At least, in my childlike eyes, I failed to win the validation from those I craved it from the most. The spirit of rejection continued to be my companion, and tried to confirm my fears of never being enough. But God! Laban eventually told Jacob to give Leah the required marriage week and then he would give him Rachel as well, while he worked another seven years... and to the dismay of Leah, Jacob agreed. So now, Leah has a week of "dutiful" relations with Jacob before she had to compete physically with Rachel. What I love about this point in Leah's life is that amid her rejection, God saw her. Genesis 29:31 says that God saw that she was unloved and moved on her behalf by opening her womb. My Sister, oh how He loves us. When the hand we are dealt seems unfair and insurmountable, when the odds are seemingly stacked against us, our Heavenly Father sees us and moves on our behalf. He is the God of a balanced weight. Just as I couldn't choose who my father would be; Leah didn't have a choice as to who her husband would be. Our God is Sovereign and He sees us and His eyes are continually beholding us (Psalm 33:18).

We now have a good perspective of Leah's situation and how the spirit of rejection was tormenting her. But there's another part that I want us to glean from. Let's continue to look at Leah's journey. Let's look at how we can, in Christ, move from a life of rejection to one of rejoicing. As Leah's plight continues, we see that despite her situation, Leah held out hope. Hope that her husband could still come to love her. She hoped that giving him sons would cause his heart to turn towards her. We see that hope in Genesis 29:32 as she named her son Reuben, (the Lord looked upon my affliction). Notice that she acknowledges that God has seen her *affliction* and shown goodness towards her, yet her heart still longed to gain the love of her husband. Still again, God allowed Leah to conceive and bear another son, she named him Simeon, (the Lord has heard). A third time, Leah conceived and bore a son, and she named him Levi (united, joined), as she hoped that Jacob's heart would be joined to her because of the fruitfulness of her womb for sons. It did not work. Don't you love how God is so patient with Leah, as He is with us? Now, up until this point, Leah's whole aim is to win the love of her husband who loved his other wife. Yet, we begin to see a change. In Genesis 29:35, we see that Leah gives birth to yet another son whom she names Judah (Praise) and she declares, *"Now I will praise the Lord!"* Hallelujah! There aren't a lot of details about exactly what happened in Leah's life between having her first son Reuben and her fourth son Judah, but what we do see is that her heart and confession has now changed. Let's take a closer look at Leah's words so that we can see the transition that happened in her heart. How do we know there has been a change? By what she said. Remember, the Bible says that *out of the abundance of the heart the mouth speaks* (Luke 6:45).

Let's follow the change. Leah's first confession was that *the Lord looked upon her affliction,* then *He heard that she was unloved*, and next, *now my husband will surely be joined to me.* In the first three births, we see that Leah acknowledges that the Lord opened her womb, but yet it does not resonate with her that He loves her and not just pities her; that He sees her and not just her affliction in being unloved by her husband. This is such a picture of how our loving Father God patiently waits for us, how even in the midst of our affliction, adversity, or disappointments, He still comes for us; working on us and on our behalf. Meanwhile, we are consumed in our situations and sometimes we miss that HE is right there with us. Why is that? I believe it's because the spirit of rejection skews our view by magnifying those who we perceive as rejecting us and minimizes those who are receiving us. We lose our peripheral vision, spiritually speaking, and we become laser focused on the rejection, which throws a boomerang that can manifest as self-doubt, low self-esteem, and self-devaluation. This, then, affects how we see; it's difficult to see ourselves as God sees us. We can become blinded in the pursuit of acceptance and forget that we have already been accepted in the Beloved (Ephesians 1:5-6).

Leah came to the place where you and I must come where, regardless of what is happening in our lives, we will praise God! Please note that Leah remained in a loveless marriage. Jacob still loved Rachel, so what changed? Leah changed along with her focus, perspective, and thus her pursuit. Leah found contentment in the blessings that the Lord had given her in her sons. What do we learn from Leah's story? We learn that regardless of our natural lot in life, when He steps in, He makes the difference as our hope is in Him (Psalm 38:15). We learn that we are loved and accepted by our heavenly Father (Ephesian 1:5-6), even when earthly parents let us down (Psalm 27:10). He sees us and is concerned about everything that concerns us (Psalm 138:8). That we find our value and purpose in Him (Acts 17:28). We learn that our Father God hears us, sees us, and loves us (Psalm 33:12-14).

Lastly, the final lesson we can glean from Leah's journey is found in Genesis 29:35b. I found this to be so powerful. It states that after the birth of Judah, Leah *"stopped giving birth"*. But we know that she eventually gave birth to three other children, Issachar, Zebulan, and Dinah. Judah ended the birthing from the womb of rejection to the womb of rejoicing! Look at Leah's confession after giving birth to her fifth son, Issachar. Genesis 30:18 says, *"God has given me my reward"* and again after her sixth son, Zebulun. Genesis 30:19 says, *"God has given me a good gift."* Once we learn that once our faith, our face, and our pursuit is towards God; giving Him the praise in all things, He will reward us. He is a rewarder of those that diligently seek him (Hebrews 11:6b). I can honestly say that once I came to a place, the reality of accepting Him that had accepted me, the spirit of rejection no longer had a hold on me. Even though it tries to raise its head periodically, especially in uncertain and unfamiliar situations, I was able, through relationship with the Lord, learning of Him, and living in the reality of His love for me, to move from the bondage of rejection to the freedom of rejoicing, and so can you!

Sarah

Stephanie Timmons, *53 years old*

"Then God said to Abraham, "As for Sarai your wife, you shall not call her name Sarai, but Sarah shall be her name." Genesis 17:15

T he past can sometimes give us insight into the future. What we can see, I chose to write about Sarah because I can relate to her in more ways than one. She teaches us about trusting God in spite of how things look with the natural eyes.

Sarah, was the wife of Abraham and left home along with her husband and went through a great deal trying to conceive and provide an heir for her husband. In the Book of Genesis, she discovered that God was in the miracle working business when she was told that she would have a child in her old age. Although God is true to His Word, Sarah didn't know how it would be done as she was old and she began to laugh. Not at God but in disbelief that it could happen for her. Not only did she laugh but she tried to help God out and take matters into her own hands.

There have been many times I've seen God move on my behalf and worked many miracles in my life. There's been times where I had to trust God and the promises He had for my life even if I, like Sarah, wanted to create a work of the flesh and produce an Ishmael instead of waiting on the promise, Isaac. One in particular, I had been a Christian for a short period of time and found myself in the emergency room of a hospital in another country where I was having an ectopic pregnancy. Basically, the baby was stuck in the tubes and ended up rupturing while I lay on a gurney in the back of the hospital as the German EMTs had taken me to the Army hospital. Upon entering the hospital, somehow, I was forgotten about and was left in a room in the back. In this time, I had only been a Christian for a little while, but realizing what had happened, I had to roll myself off the table so that someone would hear me and see about me. As I did that, nurses came running and said they didn't realize I had been brought in and as they examined me said they had to do surgery immediately or I would die. I was actually bleeding internally and had to have two blood transfusions. A day later after surgery, I was feeling as though I couldn't breathe, and after another examination, the doctors realize a sponge was left inside of me as I was bleeding internally and all they were trying to do was soak up some of the blood to do the surgery. Upon doing this, a sponge was left inside of me and away I go to have another surgery. I didn't know much but I knew that I had to Trust in the Lord according to Proverbs 3:5-6.

When God told Sarah and Abraham that they would have a child in their old age, they both laughed. As they laughed, this showed their disbelief that God could do what He said he would do. The Bible tells us,

"Then the LORD said to Abraham, 'Why did Sarah laugh and say, 'Will I really have a child, not that I am old?' Is there anything too hard for the LORD? I will return to you at the appointed time next year and Sarah will have a son.' Sarah was afraid, so she lied and said, 'I did not laugh.' But he said, 'Yes, you did laugh'" Genesis 18:13-15, NKJV.

Sometimes, God's promises are hard for us to see especially when we feel as though nothing is happening. Always know that when it appears that nothing is happening, something is always happening, even if you don't see it. Abraham fell on his face in worship and God did bless them and do exactly what He said He would do even in Sarah's old age.

SARAH

God promised Sarah and Abraham children and when this didn't take place as quickly as they thought it should have, they became impatient with God and took matters into their own hands. Sarah told Abraham to sleep with her handmaid so that they could have a child from this union. Not long after, a son was born from them and his name was Ishamel, which means work for the flesh. This was not God's divine plan for their life as God had promised (Isaac) because through Isaac, the nation would be blessed. Sometimes, the plans that we have are not always God's plans and we need to totally surrender and trust God in everything. After all, He said He would make our paths straight if we trust Him and lean not to our own understanding. Yes, sometimes it's hard, but without Faith it's impossible to please Him. We don't always see how it's going to happen, but he does.

About a year and a half after my first major ordeal as a believer, I found myself in another dire situation where I had to trust and believe the God of the Word that I had been reading about day in and day out. I went to the doctor because I had trouble with my sight and was told that I had glaucoma. Not only did I have glaucoma, but the optometrist also told me that I was in the 3rd stage and in one more stage, I would have been considered legally blind soon. My husband and I went home, found our faith in the Word of God, and began to speak what He spoke according to Isaiah 53:5:

"But he was wounded for our transgressions, he was bruised for our iniquities: the chastisement of our peace was upon him; and with his stripes we are healed."

I went back to the doctor and he did the examination and said he needed to do it again as he doesn't misdiagnose patients. After looking again, he said he didn't realize what had happened, but I actually had 20/20 vision. God had done what He said he was going to do according to His Word. By His stripes, I was truly healed. God truly does love us and wants us to live by His Word. Ultimately, our faith will produce the promises He has for us if we trust and believe. Sometimes, we may face infertility in our lives. We have to realize that this is not punishment. Sometimes, it is protection from other things that may transpire later on. According to Romans 8:28, it says: *"And we know that all things work together for good to them that love God, to them who are the called according to his purpose."*

Many of us struggle with not being able to conceive and this could lead to all kinds of feelings to include depression, and some may even wonder if this is some sort of punishment. Truth be told, God is not punishing us if we are having trouble having a baby. While we may not understand the plans that are unfolding before us, just like Sarah, it's not our plan to question. God's timing is not always ours and ultimately, He sees the end before the beginning and perhaps He may be calling us to adopt, or foster a child or children. He may also be calling us to a place of Goshen, which is drawing nigh unto Him.

However, in the midst of it all, God loves us in spite of us. Remember how I shared that Abraham and Sarah laughed at God when He told them they would conceive a child in their old age. Well, although they laughed and they then took matters into their own hands, God never held that against them. God loves us even when we try to help Him out. Just as God loves them, He loves us, too. We've all been there and have made bad choices but God says He is faithful and just to cleanse us from all unrighteousness. All we have to do is repent and get right back on track.

Sometimes, we find ourselves in the same position as Sarah. We may not think that our lives line up with hers, but in a lot of ways, we have a lot more in common than we think with Sarah. We all have a vision for our lives. We grow up, we go to college, we get married, and think our lives are supposed to go a certain way. We sometimes get caught up in trying to figure out what God has already worked out. We have to completely trust God with our lives and totally surrender unto Him and as we do, He will certainly guide us with His eyes.

Mary the Sister of Martha

Emily Powless, *31 years old*

> "Now it happened as they went that He entered a certain village; and a certain woman named Martha welcomed Him into her house. And she had a sister called Mary,..." Luke 10:38-42

Lou Engle says, "There comes a time when you go for broke when the treasure is so great, you sell everything you have to buy the field. Jesus is the treasure in the field." This statement Lou Engle made has directed so many launching moments in my family's life. Matthew 13:44-45 is my favorite scripture in the entire Bible. God has spoken to me in so many different ways through it. It reads, *"The kingdom of heaven is like a treasure hidden in the field, which a man hid again, and from joy over it he goes and sells all he has to buy the field. Again, the kingdom of heaven is like a merchant seeking fine pearls, and upon finding one pearl of great value, he went and sold all that he had, and bought it. Where your treasure is, that's where your heart will be."*

Right now, I want you to stop reading and ponder what comes to your mind when I say, "treasure." Maybe it's a box filled with gold, silver, and precious jewels. It could be a new vehicle, or a larger house. What about a brand-new diamond ring? A pay raise. It could even be a spouse, children, or parents. The world defines these things as *treasures*, and none are inherently evil, yet so many of these things block our view of the ultimate treasure. Jesus is THE treasure. Many items, I would deem as treasures in my lifetime, have come and left as quickly as they came, yet Jesus has remained faithful when everything else in my life fell apart. God has never left or forsaken me, even when trials didn't go the way I'd assumed. He has even been merciful in walking me through forgiveness, healing, and deliverance. So many people get fixated on material items and will spend their entire lives trying to obtain all the world says is necessary for happiness. When it just steals our money and our time.

What if we quit viewing physical items like treasures, instead of resources like they actually are? When I get in the presence of my Savior, everything else completely melts away. Peace rushes in, and the Comforter is in the atmosphere. The chaos ceases, and the worry melts away, and I find myself just weeping at His feet for His goodness and mercy, not because of what I've done, but for what He already did. My personal wants become so insignificant once I get into His presence. My needs begin to come into their proper alignment, and I can see His hand and His blessings in my life, even if I am not getting what I want. Every dream, ambition, title, and work I have strived to obtain becomes useless if my treasure wasn't Jesus. All the righteousness I could muster up in myself is like filthy rags as the scriptures say, compared to the right-eousness of my King. His blood is what made me righteous, not my works. I could spend my entire life creating a name for myself as the world tells me to do, and it would be useless when I stand before God. I could do many things for Him, yet never truly know Him. Intimacy requires proximity. We can't be intimate with our Savior when treasures continuously sit higher than Him. Mary chose intimacy. She understood that His presence was more valuable than her duties. Mary wasn't slothful, but she understood the hour of her visitation was at hand. Mary sat at the feet of Jesus three separate times in Scripture, and she gleaned from every single word that proceeded from His mouth. She marveled at His glory and His majesty, and she decided to be still and sit at Jesus' feet, despite the cost, despite the judgment people probably gave her afterward. She didn't care about her name or her reputation. She just wanted to listen to what Jesus was speaking. She found the treasure in the field, and she locked eyes on the prize, and on that day, she had a made-up mind that He was worth it. In the societal standard, it would have been unheard of for Mary to sit at Jesus' feet in the first place.

Typically, the father (since she was unmarried) would hear the message, and later reiterate what was taught by the Rabbi. Women would not have the opportunity to hear firsthand, but Mary heard it straight from the source. She defied all the cultural norms to press into her Savior and listen to His words straight from His mouth. She had a hunger. She didn't want to do what was good, but she wanted to do what her spirit longed for. She didn't care what others thought, even her sister. We know the story. Martha was busy with many things as the Bible says, but she was just doing the customary womanly duties. The tasks she was partaking in weren't inherently bad at all, she just didn't realize the hour of visitation that was before her like Mary did. She wanted to be a good host. She was annoyed that everything fell on her shoulders. At some point, every mother has felt like Martha before. Martha gets a bad rap but we have all been a Martha in some way or another in our walks with God. From preparing church dinners to programs, facilitating worship, or being in leadership positions inside the Church.

We can become so busy that we know Jesus is in the room, but we have a task in our minds that simply cannot be put off. As women, we usually feel idle hands are a negative trait, but we must rest in His presence to get filled back up. We cannot pour from an empty cup. If as women we aren't resting at our Savior's feet, we are usually burning the candle on both ends. We will not have the peace or the tenacity to accomplish any task, especially when we are operating in the flesh versus the Spirit. Like Martha, we all want to be a good host in the natural, but are we intentional with hosting Him in every aspect of life, even the vulnerable areas? Many believers are distracted by things that spring up out of nowhere and scream for our immediate attention, but we must take time to heal. A good distraction will keep us from entering into His presence, but we must push it aside and be intentional in our relationship with God. It must take priority. The distraction can appear good, but that doesn't mean it's godly. Not everything that screams needs your immediate focus either. Even my children know when I am spending time in prayer that whatever they want can generally wait. They will usually enter in prayer/worship with me, hug me and play, or quietly step away until I am finished unless it is an emergency. Many in the Church think that their many works equate to holiness. We should serve, but where is our heart in the serving? Martha was poisoned with her sister. Her heart posture was seeking justification for her offense from Jesus. Where is our heart posture? Are we coming to Jesus with our complaints or our worship? Many will talk to God about their problems, but unfortunately not as many just want to hear His voice. It's hard to hear God if you won't stop long enough to listen to the words that He is speaking. Many get on the "merry-go-round" of doing good deeds for Him, but they lack the oil. The oil cannot be earned or deserved. It comes from being filled up with it, in His presence. We cannot pour out on others what we haven't cultivated inside by being intimate with the Father.

The scriptures speak of Mary sitting at Jesus' feet on three separate occasions to learn, at His feet when Lazarus passed away, and the third time pouring the expensive oil on His feet and washing it with her hair. There is something so powerful about being at the feet of Jesus in a humble position. Mary understood the importance of worshipping Jesus in all situations of her life. What a beautiful testimony that we can apply to our lives. Mary loved Jesus. Her life showed how reverent He was to her. Even when she couldn't understand Lazarus' situation, she still sat at Jesus' feet. How many of us would have complained? She simply said, "Lord, if you had been here, my brother would not have died." In distress, she still fell at His feet. Jesus was deeply moved in the Spirit by compassion. Jesus wept for what Mary wept for. Then, we know Lazarus was resurrected. This foreshadowed Jesus' death, but it was also a trial for Mary. She still believed and had faith in Him, even when things did not go her way. There was something so pure and extravagant in her worship when she took the pound of expensive perfume, which was pure nard, then used it to anoint His feet; this time, she wasn't there to receive, but to pour out. Jesus was more important to her than her most expensive treasures on Earth. She anointed His feet with this sacred oil that was used for a wedding night to anoint the martial bed. King Solomon speaks of spikenard with his beloved bride. This is a prophetic representation of how intimate and infatuated we are to be with our Lord, not weirdly or lustfully, but in pure intimacy and relationship with God. We are the Bride of Christ.

Intimacy is in admiration and fellowship, but also unconditional love. The price of spikenard was so high that kings would use it as expensive perfumes and ointments. Cleopatra used spikenard with other oils to create her perfumes that were fit for royalty. King Tut was even found buried with spikenard oil. Judas references that she could have sold it to the poor for 300 denarii, which according to Matthew 20:2 was an entire day's wage. That would equate to 300 days' worth of work for many people. It was worth it to Mary. She wiped His feet with the precious oil because He was worthy. Using her tears and her hair, she poured everything she had on Him. Oil fit for the kings and queens of this world was poured on the ultimate King of Kings. I can only imagine how pleased the Father was with Mary. She was preparing Jesus for His burial, but she also poured out what He had already cultivated inside of her. We see John the Beloved rest on Jesus' bosom, and that is where we should be as His Bride as well, resting in His presence. Mary loved Jesus, and Jesus loved Mary. Jesus loves His Church. Jesus loves His Bride and He's returning soon like a Galilean wedding to retrieve her. I ask you today, have you allowed Him to pour into you so that you can, in return, pour back your love and admiration to Him? Martha was busy with works, distracted, and offended by her sister. Judas was offended that she "wasted" the precious oil on the Lord and didn't give the money to the poor. Lavishing love and admiration offends lukewarmness and religion. Yet she pushed in despite her reputation to get filled up with the Word. She fell on her face weeping and rubbing oil on our precious Savior's feet with her hair before His feet and hands were nailed to the Cross. She understood that Jesus was the ultimate treasure.

Despite the physical cost of her treasure, it was nothing compared to what Jesus gave us, eternal life. What on this Earth is more precious than the blood of Jesus covering every single sin? His blood covers all sickness, trauma, and pain. His blood is stronger than any mental stronghold and is stronger than any demonic force. His blood reversed the curse and brought us back into perfect alignment with the Father. We can now walk and talk with Him as Adam did in the Garden. We can intimately know Him. The veil has been torn, and we can boldly go before Him. He chose to die for us. Can we choose to live our lives to glorify Him? Is He your treasure or do you go to Him asking for treasures of this world? Is He worth selling it all for? Is He worth spending everything on? Is He worth staying at His feet when we don't understand why things are happening the way they are? Is He worth it to you? In a world that is full of Marthas, be a Mary.

Jael

Blakeley Jael Powless, *10 years old*

"Most blessed among women is Jael, the wife of Heber the Kenite; Blessed is she among women in tents." Judges 5:24

Jael holds a very special place in my heart. My mom named me Jael. Many years I spent trying to measure up to such a powerful person in the Bible. I always thought I had to strive for perfection and be a strong warrior, but once I relaxed and accepted my identity as a child of God, I found stepping into my identity was easy. I realized I have many characteristics like her. I am strong, smart, and I don't give up easily. I fight for what is right, despite the push back I get.

When I was in public school, I stood up and didn't participate in yoga, and I didn't partake of many things other kids did. I was kind and compassionate, but strong in what I would stand for. Despite everyone doing it, I couldn't bow down to things that God convicted me of. I realized I am not a woman called to stab someone with a tent peg, but God has shown me I am called to be a Teacher. I can be strong and stand for what is right, but what was right for Jael in the Bible, doesn't mean that's exactly how God has called me to be.

An interesting thing about Jael is that her name means "mountain goat," and to be useful. I used to get very embarrassed by this. I realized that's what my name meant, but it seems kind of weird. Then, I realized characteristics of a mountain goat are intelligent and fearless. They are able to adapt to harsh conditions, and they rarely lose their balance. Jael was also very useful not only for herself, but for an entire nation.

Jael's story is very powerful. She wasn't always a warrior, but a wife. I can't relate to that, but I can relate to being raised up in a home, wanting purpose and having to be obedient, despite being very willful. Here is the entire story of Jael in Judges 4:

"Again the Israelites did evil in the eyes of the LORD, now that Ehud was dead. So the LORD sold them into the hands of Jabin, king of Canaan, who reigned in Hazor. Sisera, the commander of his army, was based in Harosheth Haggoyim. Because he had nine hundred chariots fitted with iron and had cruelly oppressed the Israelites for twenty years, they cried to the LORD for help. Now Deborah, a prophet, the wife of Lappidoth, was leading Israel at that time. She held court under the Palm of Deborah between Ramah and Bethel in the hill country of Ephraim, and the Israelites went up to her to have their disputes decided. She sent for Barak son of Abinoam from Kedesh in Naphtali and said to him, "The LORD, the God of Israel, commands you: 'Go, take with you ten thousand men of Naphtali and Zebulun and lead them up to Mount Tabor. I will lead Sisera, the commander of Jabin's army, with his chariots and his troops to the Kishon River and give him into your hands.'" Barak said to her, "If you go with me, I will go; but if you don't go with me, I won't go." "Certainly I will go with you," said Deborah. "But because of the course you are taking, the honor will not be yours, for the LORD will deliver Sisera into the hands of a woman." So Deborah went with Barak to Kedesh. There Barak summoned Zebulun and Naphtali, and ten thousand men went up under his command. Deborah also went up with him. Now Heber the Kenite had left the other Kenites, the descendants of Hobab, Moses' brother-in-law, and pitched his tent by the great tree in Zaanannim near Kedesh. When they told Sisera that Barak son of Abinoam had gone up to Mount Tabor, Sisera summoned from Harosheth Haggoyim to the Kishon River all his men and his nine hundred chariots fitted with iron. Then Deborah said to Barak, "Go! This is the day the LORD has given Sisera into your hands. Has not the LORD gone ahead of you?" So Barak went down

JAEL

Mount Tabor, with ten thousand men following him. At Barak's advance, the LORD routed Sisera and all his chariots and army by the sword, and Sisera got down from his chariot and fled on foot. Barak pursued the chariots and army as far as Harosheth Haggoyim, and all Sisera's troops fell by the sword; not a man was left. Sisera, meanwhile, fled on foot to the tent of Jael, the wife of Heber the Kenite, because there was an alliance between Jabin king of Hazor and the family of Heber the Kenite. Jael went out to meet Sisera and said to him, "Come, my lord, come right in. Don't be afraid." So he entered her tent, and she covered him with a blanket. "I'm thirsty," he said. "Please give me some water." She opened a skin of milk, gave him a drink, and covered him up. "Stand in the doorway of the tent," he told her. "If someone comes by and asks you, 'Is anyone in there?' say 'No.'" But Jael, Heber's wife, picked up a tent peg and a hammer and went quietly to him while he lay fast asleep, exhausted. She drove the peg through his temple into the ground, and he died. Just then Barak came by in pursuit of Sisera, and Jael went out to meet him. "Come," she said, "I will show you the man you're looking for." So he went in with her, and there lay Sisera with the tent peg through his temple—dead. On that day God subdued Jabin king of Canaan before the Israelites. And the hand of the Israelites pressed harder and harder against Jabin, king of Canaan until they destroyed him."

I wrote a poem like they did in Judges 5. It was my inspiration to write this:

Jael was a warrior
When all that was thought was just a blur
You would not believe what she would stir
There was a prophecy that a woman would win
Even against a bad nation then
We all want to be like them but we don't want to count the cost
Too much is at stake even winning the lost
Israel was saved by a woman that day
All she had to do was simply obey
Get in Christ and He will set you free
Step up and be the woman you are called to be

We should all want to be like Jael, in regard that she was obedient to God. Not that we want people to know about us, but that we do what God tells us to do. We have to have a relationship with God in order to do what He has spoken for us to do. Don't say "I'm just a woman," say *I'm a warrior for God*, that can be in prayer or even physically. Women are strong when they trust in God.

Women need to step into their destiny. Jael had a purpose for that time and so do you now. She had to step into being a warrior. Her entire life was prepared for that moment. The woman at the well was the first woman evangelist. Ruth was faithful; she left everything to follow Naomi. Mary sat at Jesus' feet and just listened to Him. Deborah was a prophet and prophesied about Israel. Tabitha cared for people and made clothes for them. Esther was brave, she went up to the king and saved her people. You may ask, What can I do as a woman? Anything God tells you to do.

You have so much purpose inside of you. You may not be the next Jael, Deborah, or Esther, but you are created by God for God. He has a plan for your life, and that plan is to help people know Him. We are given characteristics by God so that He can use us in the way He created us, to touch others. You were born to the right parents, in the right town, on the right day, because God needed you here for right now. Everything you have gone through is to prepare you for something someone needs. Your testimony and giftings, used properly, will point others back to Jesus. Maybe you are called to teach kid's class or women. Step into it. You may be called to be a missionary, go. You may be called to sing and be a worshipper, just sing and dance before your king. Maybe you are called to be a prayer warrior.

Jael saved an entire nation by her simple obedience to God. What is God calling you to do? What has God placed inside of you for others? Ask God, "What do you want me to do for You? Then, watch and see how amazing of an adventure it is going to be.

The Woman

With the Issue of Blood

Amy Tisdale, *45 years old*

"And suddenly, a woman who had a flow of blood for twelve years came from behind and touched the hem of His garment." Mark 9:20

October 10, 2021 started out like any other Sunday. I went to church, and enjoyed time with family and friends in the hours that followed. That evening was far from normal. I was relaxing on my sofa and had a massive stroke. I did not realize what was happening in that moment. Thankfully, my husband walked into the room and saw me slumped over. He immediately knew what was happening and contacted emergency services. They arrived and immediately transported me to the hospital. I had to be transferred to a different hospital to receive the care I needed though. Once I was out of that first surgery, we learned more about what was going on. My future was very uncertain. I was left with semi-paralysis on my left side and some slight cognitive disabilities. My physical impairments left me unable to walk without an adaptive device or to use my left arm and hand. I underwent seven brain surgeries and months of intense rehabilitation to learn to start walking. Most medical professionals left us with no hope I would recover full use of my left arm or hand. So many times after that, I thought about the woman who touched the hem of Jesus's garment and was instantly healed. I cried out for that same chance. In a quiet whisper within my heart, God reminded me.

This story is about the woman's total faith in Him, not about the actual touching of the garment's hem. I've had to ask myself, "Do I have faith He will heal me even if it isn't an immediate healing?" I absolutely know I am known and loved by my Creator. Nothing has touched my life without first going through His hands.

"In Him we also have obtained an inheritance, having been predestined according to the purpose of Him who works all things in accordance with the plan of His will" Ephesians 1:11, ESV.

Maybe, just maybe, my healing isn't supposed to be an immediate physical healing, but a spiritual healing from wounds that run deep from hurt by others I've let take hold in my heart. God has been using these past years to make Himself far more personal to me than I've ever let Him. He's been healing me from fears of being hurt while showing His sovereignty in all things that come my way.

The Woman with the Issue of Blood had suffered with this disorder for twelve years and doctors had been unable to heal her. By Jewish law, she was considered unclean and anyone who came into physical contact with her would be deemed unclean, as well. She was desperate for a miracle. Her touching Jesus did not make Him unclean but made her fully clean. Likewise, our sin makes us unclean, but our complete faith in our Savior makes us fully clean. God begins working/moving upon our faith in Him. I am still waiting on my complete healing, but I am holding onto faith that it is coming. I may never fully understand why my faith hasn't healed me completely in a physical sense, but I know a spiritual healing has occurred and is beyond greater than the physical healing I still desperately desire.

"And there was a woman who had had a discharge of blood for twelve years, and who had suffered much under many physicians, and had spent all that she had, and was no better but rather grew worse. She had heard the reports about Jesus and came up behind him in the crowd

and touched his garment. For she said, "If I touch even his garments, I will be made well." And immediately the flow of blood dried up, and she felt in her body that she was healed of her disease. And Jesus, perceiving in himself that power had gone out from him, immediately turned about in the crowd and said, "Who touched my garments?" And his disciples said to him, "You see the crowd pressing around you, and yet you say, 'Who touched me?'" And he looked around to see who had done it. But the woman, knowing what had happened to her, came in fear and trembling and fell down before him and told him the whole truth. And he said to her, "Daughter, your faith has made you well; go in peace, and be healed of your disease" Mark 5:25-34, ESV.

The season of waiting I am currently in requires faith, and trusting His plan is better than mine. Trusting God's plan is difficult when so much has not been made known. This woman did not know for a fact she would be healed, yet she went to see Jesus anyway. While He may not remove the difficulties immediately, He will and does help us through them. He ultimately knows what is best for us, and we are called to trust Him. We must keep the faith. I believe one day God will whisper quietly to me once again, but He will say,

"Daughter, your faith has made you well; go in peace and be healed of your disease" Mark 5:34, ESV.

Priscilla

Angie Baldwin, *45 years old*

"The churches of Asia greet you. Aquila and Priscilla greet you heartily in the Lord, with the church that is in their house." 1 Corinthians 16:19

In 2010, my husband came into the bedroom with a serious and contemplative look. He seemed to be wrestling with something great and his gaze informed me that he was seeking my full attention. I had been rocking our newborn baby girl, Rosalyn, to sleep. I carefully placed her down in her cradle, praying that she would not wake up from her slumber. After a few more quiet minutes to ensure she was finding rest, I looked up at him. He took my hand and said to me quietly, "I have been asked to take another church appointment." I wasn't surprised as my husband was a gifted speaker, teacher, and pastor. Besides, I will admit that I was more than willing to leave our current assignment. It had been turbulent and an extremely unhappy experience for me and our two older girls. It was as if God were sending a lifeboat to us and I was so joyful for its arrival! I tried to stay solemn on the outside but inwardly, I was on my knees in tears, praising and thanking God!

"And he found a certain Jew named Aquila, born in Pontus, who had recently come from Italy with his wife Priscilla (because Claudius had commanded all the Jews to depart from Rome); and he came to them" Acts 18:2.

Priscilla and her husband, Aquila, were faithful believers and traveled frequently sharing the Gospel with people far and wide, but their departure from Rome was not initially a family decision, yet one they were forced to endure. For my husband and I, we would soon find ourselves in a very similar situation. My heart and nearly my spirit had been broken in this place of assignment. We were still very young in ministry. We were only in our twenties, and new to being a pastoral family. Our very first church was a lovely, small congregation, and having grown up in a small church, I was well adapted to deal with the needs and to engage with this congregation as a Pastor's wife. There were county picnics, scriptural teachings and community engagement, and a reinfused gospel choir, who traveled with us whenever my husband preached. Most importantly, this church was a community of believers. I loved them and there were tears when he was sent away after three years. However, my husband had finished his Master of Divinity degree and was ready for his next assignment reassigned. In the beginning I had such hopes and dreams of community and social engagement at our new church. I thought, ideally, that God was placing us there to have a great move of God to come about. One that would affect not only the people in the congregation, but the community as well. Little did I know that all the hopes and dreams that I had for our next appointment would become null and void.

As after this next move, never in our lives were my husband and I so mentally terrorized, lied on, and spiritually attacked. You see, Satan often seeks out those he can use to diminish and destroy for his purpose. No matter how hard they tried, not many people were convinced to think evil of us; nothing could divide us from our marriage vows and from Godly principles. That attack having failed, the next best thing was to convince as many people as possible that we, as a couple, had indeed strayed from morality and were lost in a life of chaos, adultery, and disorder. This vile spread far and wide. The people who wished to believe the worst… well, they did. However, those who truly knew my husband and I, as well as those who were convicted by the Holy Spirit that there was no truth in the rumors, just prayed harder for us. Looking back, I feel so sorry for those who received the luring of Satan time and time again. We must forgive, release them, and give them to God.

We must understand that not all churches are built on the foundation of the true Gospel. I know we all want to believe the best but we cannot be ignorant to the truth that we have a real enemy whose desire is to taint and pervert the true, authentic Gospel of our Lord Jesus Christ. The Bible says not to be ignorant of the devices of Satan. He will send people as well; he will plant his workers in our houses of Worship to destroy the work of Christ. In these deceptive times we are currently living in, this is happening more than we would like to admit yet as we are filled with the precious Holy Spirit, He will give us keen discernment to know who is of Him and who is not. Seek the voice of Holy Spirit so you and your family are not deceived in these end times.

"... lest Satan should take advantage of us; for we are not ignorant of his devices" 2 Corinthians 2:11 and *"Do not be deceived, my beloved brethren..."* James 1:16.

Persecution was given to us much like that of the Romans, to Priscilla and Aquila. However, unlike Priscilla, at this time, I lacked the experience and humility that shone throughout her life. I was so deadened and broken that I allowed my desire to really work, uplift, and make a difference in this appointed Body of Christ to be vanquished. I receded and my light and God given gifts were hidden away. As we purpose to live the scriptures and understand the devices of our enemy, we are better equipped to stand in the midst of great persecution and attacks. We will be able to boldly stand in the face of our enemy and lift up the light and life of our Lord, Jesus Christ.

"Where in North Carolina are we being sent?" I remember cautiously asking him. My husband took my hand, "No, not anywhere in North Carolina, but to serve in Louisiana. I need you to pray about it." Then, he left me to ponder this news. I was not surprised, but surely taken aback at the confirmation of several clues that had led up to this revelation. For one, the movie *Princess and the Frog*, which celebrated New Orleans, had captured our hearts. Secondly, some months before, the pull of the Holy Spirit had led me to purchase a large, hardback book that spoke of the history and cuisine of Louisiana. Finally, and the most foretelling of them all, was that our home address was on Bourbon Street. So, after an hour or so of contemplating this move of God and all the things that needed to be done; I was quite settled upon going. There were family members and close friends we had to acquaint with the news. Sadly, we knew the hardest people this information would hit were my husband's father and my dear mother. I don't think either of them had envisioned this type of move happening. Nor us for being so ready to leave our beautiful and ancestral home state.

"And He said to them, "Go into all the world and preach the gospel to every creature" Mark 16:15.

I was also diagnosed with Multiple Sclerosis when I was 24, and having my mom, sister, and brother close was essential. There was also my husband's maternal family who had to see their late sister's only son depart from their reach. Uncle Thomas, who worked as a guard at the entrance of our gated community, would often see our 9-year-old daughter get on and off the bus and make it safely to our house. With Uncle Thomas, we knew if any emergency would arise, he could simply take her home with him and to his wife, Aunt Mary, at least until my mother, or we, could retrieve her. With a move to unfamiliar territory, we would have no such guarantees and with a newborn baby and an additional 4-year-old daughter, we had to put all trust in God.

"So Paul still remained a good while. Then he took leave of the brethren and sailed for Syria, and Priscilla and Aquila were with him" Acts 18:18.

Like Priscilla, I had to go where I was sent with my husband, and just believe that God had already arranged adopted family for us. Oh my, and so did He! In these years, He has given us Louisiana family that we can only praise God for! He knitted us with another Mary who my kids fondly call "Ma Mary!" and another Louisiana cooking Grandma, "Sister Billie," both of whom adore our children. He sent us angels in the form of neighbors, school and athletic parents, co-workers, and law enforcement who have become family to us. They watched over the safety of our family, kids, and even me during my MS relapses. Then, in 2015, we were delighted to welcome another addition to our family! A baby boy was born in New Orleans. When our daughter Rosalyn was called as a child to go out to the nation, these people got behind her, and us as a family, to support. My husband has served our current congregation, going on ten years. The icing on the top was that God so blessed us for our current church to have the same name as our very first congregation. They are our family, indeed! Our current church family has been the grandfathers, grandmothers, aunts, and uncles to our children and dearest kinsmen to us! Therefore, our children have grown up as *Louisiana kids* and are finding their way as God leads them on a fabulous path to many current and future lifelong successes.

I want to speak to the pastors, preachers, ministers, missionaries, evangelists, and all those sent out to the nations of the world to preach the Gospel. You will, indeed, face many obstacles, many attacks, many persecutions, as you obey the voice of the Lord to "go into all the world and preach the Gospel to every creature," but be encouraged—He has equipped and empowered you to walk through *the fiery furnaces*, to stand boldly in *the Lion's Den*, and to even *humbly serve your accusers and forgive them* as our Lord, Jesus Christ did in the midst of His own persecution. See, the enemy's desire is to stifle and even destroy your witness in the Earth realm through the evil spirit of offense and the attacks of your enemies, but keep in mind, the Word of God reminds us that we do not wrestle with mere human beings, but a greater foe that is hellbent on destroying Christ's image within us.

"For we do not wrestle against flesh and blood, but against principalities, against powers, against the rulers of the darkness of this age, against spiritual hosts of wickedness in the heavenly places" Ephesians 6:12.

Priscilla and Aquila faced many persecutions as they accepted the call to *GO*, and we, too, will face them as we obey that still small voice of our Heavenly Father, whispering to us our destiny calling. Just know that as you obey, He will provide everything you need to fulfill the assignment He has predestined for you.

All I can say is, "Thank You, God!" He kept us through the storm and continues to cover us with His anointing and we shall continue to stay true to God's direction and path. Amen!

Eunice

Juanita E. Davis, *53 years old*

"When I call to remembrance the genuine faith that is in you, which dwelt first in your grandmother Lois and your mother Eunice, and I am persuaded is in you also." 2 Timothy 1:5

Eunice: Joyous, Victorious.

The only mention of Timothy's mother, Eunice, in the Bible is in that one verse, but it is not a verse that is to be quickly read over or to be taken lightly. For the mother, grandmother, or any believer that desires to leave a legacy for their children, it is powerful. When the Apostle Paul wrote of Eunice, he wrote not only about her faith but also about her *genuine* faith. According to E-Sword's Bible Dictionary, genuine in that verse means "*undissembled*, that is sincere: without dissimulation (hypocrisy), unfeigned." In other words, Eunice's faith in God was unwavering and was one that revealed that she totally depended on God and took Him at His every word. It was one that said that she was not all over the place in her belief in Him but stood rooted and grounded in, and with feet firmly planted upon, the solid rock of Jesus. It was that same type of faith, according to the apostle's writing, that her mother Lois had possessed and passed on to her daughter, and both of them to Timothy. Talk about a legacy!

Until I finally stopped and read this verse, and stopped reading over it, I had only thought of a family legacy as the passing down of a business, a family fortune, or some other tangible inheritance. I also thought that it was usually a male family member that the inheritance originated with and was passed down from. However, when I took the time to read this verse and to study the background of it, I realized that the greatest legacy my husband Randy and I can pass on to our sons and their children is one of faith—a genuine, sincere, undissembled, unfeigned, and unwavering faith in God, just as Lois and Eunice had passed on to Timothy.

Speaking of the inheritance or legacy originating with and being passed down from a male family member, where was Timothy's father or even his grandfather; and why did the apostle not mention either of them? There is actually no mention of Timothy's grandfather nor his father in the entire Bible. Some speculate that his father was not a believer, while others speculate that he was deceased. Being that all Scripture is God-breathed and given by inspiration of the Holy Spirit, what if God did this on purpose? What if He purposely did not inspire the apostle to mention a father or a grandfather, not because they lacked importance but to speak to the heart of grandmothers and mothers in the Church? After all, it is not just in the world, but in the Church too, where we see grandmothers and mothers raising grandsons and sons in the absence of grandfathers and fathers. I once found myself ministering this very verse as encouragement to a young unmarried mother of four. She had never been married and felt that she could not successfully raise her children (especially her sons) without a father to help guide them according to the Word of God. Taking her to the scriptures, I was led to point out to her that in his letter to Timothy, the Apostle Paul made no mention of a grandfather or father—only of Timothy's grandmother and mother—and that he commended Timothy for pos-sessing the same genuine faith that they had.

The message to her was that with the Lord, she, too, could pass on a legacy of genuine faith to all of her children. This in no way was intended to diminish the role or the importance of having a father in the home, but what do we say to the women just like that single mother that I had ministered to, or the widow who has been left to raise her children without their father, or the divorcee, the Christian mother who is married to an unbeliever, or the military moms like myself whose husbands were gone for sometimes months at a time, or worked odd hours due to the demands of their jobs?

That same message that I had shared with that young mother was one that Holy Spirit had ministered to me, years earlier, when my husband was an active-duty airman in the Air Force. All glory to God, my own experience was what He used to help me relate to the unmarried mother's situation to a degree, but enough to be able to minister effectively and with understanding to her. I had separated from the Air Force shortly after our first of four sons was born. That decision was made prayerfully and based on the fact that my husband and I both had highly deployable and very demanding jobs, and we believed that having me at home full-time would help in the way of offering stability to our son and any future children that we might have. My husband possessed and still possesses that same type of genuine faith that Lois and Eunice did, but his job kept him away from home a lot due to shift variances or deployments. Most of the time, although he was at home or in town, he would be asleep when our sons awoke for the day and would have already left for work when they returned home from school. That left my sons and me spending a whole lot of time together—me with my emotional moments and them with their mood swings as they morphed into tweens, teens, and eventually young men.

As crises arose over the years, I knew that I had to get a rein on my emotions and show them what genuine faith in God looked like. Despite why their father was not there, the reality was that I was the one whom my sons spent most of their time with. Due to that fact, I wanted to be just as effective in adding to their faith as their father was; and him and me being faith builders together for them as Lois and Eunice were for Timothy. The last thing that my sons needed was mixed messages. I was the one whose reactions, or responses, they would see when those crises like phone calls with bad reports, one or all of them misbehaving, or any other crisis that arose in those times when my husband could not be there like he, they, *we* wanted. The decision that I had to make, regardless of how stressed or overwhelmed I sometimes felt, was to respond in godly wisdom and in sincere faith. If I told them that God was able and that He could fix whatever problem there was, I needed to show it. If I told them that He could and would provide regardless of how big the need was, I needed to show it. If I told them *yes* or *no* to something that they wanted or wanted to do, then I needed to let my *yes be yes* and my *no be no*. It was imperative to not only the family legacy of genuine faith that my husband and I desired to pass on to them, but also to their spiritual well-being that I stood without wavering. Regardless to how little time our sons got to spend with their father, his faith in God preceded him; and they saw it. Therefore, it was imperative that my life published the same message as my husband's before our sons.

Early on in my walk, I had a conversation with my pastor at the time. In that conversation, I told him that the legacy that I desired to pass on to my children was a financial legacy. After all, that is what I had heard about so often as I was growing up; and it sounded really good and honorable. In truth, it is biblical and therefore right. However, my pastor, who was the father of three young children, looked at me very intently, smiled, and replied with, "Nita, how about letting the greatest legacy that you want to pass on to your children be faith?" He did not diminish the importance of a financial legacy, he only challenged me (by the Spirit of God) to re-prioritize; and from that moment on, my perspective, as well as my priorities, changed. Although I still do want to pass on a financial legacy, or inheritance, to my children, the greatest legacy that I have desired from that conversation is to pass on a legacy of faith and trust in the Lord to them. The marvelous thing about this is that with the financial legacy, they have to wait until I die and leave this Earth for it to pass on to them, but with the legacy of faith, it gets passed on every time my faith is tested and I choose to die to self and model genuine faith in God before them.

I began this devotional by sharing the biblical meaning of Eunice's name: joyous and victorious. These meanings are key for not only the so-named Eunice's of the world, but also for anyone that desires to have genuine faith and to pass it on as a legacy to their children and their children's children. Joy is not contingent upon happenings, nor does it occur from time to time. It is not a joyous-one-minute-then-sad-and-miserable-the-next roller coaster of emotions. Instead, it originates from our Lord, and He desires that it be constant and ongoing in spite of what is happening around, to, in, or about us. *"Rejoice in the Lord always. I will say it again. Rejoice!"* Secondly, genuine faith always proves victorious. Why? Because the possessor of genuine faith fights from a vantage point *of* victory, not *for* victory. That vantage point is Christ, in Whom we dwell and put our faith; and with Him on our side and us on His, victory is guaranteed. That is, victory according to His definition of it, not ours.

Joy and victory were the very message that the Apostle Paul was trying to convey to Timothy in 2 Timothy 1. When he wrote the letter to Timothy, Paul was in prison—not for anything that he had done wrong, but for preaching the Gospel. Due to that fact, he was encouraging Timothy to not shrink back from preaching the Gospel due to fear of being imprisoned, or worse, but to instead "stir up the gift of God" in himself, which was imparted to him through Paul laying hands on the younger preacher. Paul preceded that encouragement by telling Timothy that he was praying for him night and day and that he was aware of his tears. He then went on to tell him that he remembered the genuine faith of Timothy, that same genuine faith that was in his grandmother and mother first and that was sure to also be in him.

Despite Timothy's tears and his fears, the Apostle Paul was encouraging Timothy to dig his heels in deep and to exercise that *undissembled, sincere:* without dissimulation (hypocrisy), unfeigned, genuine faith that he believed the young preacher to possess. To you my fellow *Daughter of Destiny*, I encourage you to do the same in order that the legacy of genuine faith will either continue to be, or start to be, passed on through you from generation to generation!

Tamar

Angie Wynn, *59 years old*

"After this Absalom the son of David had a lovely sister, whose
name was Tamar; and Amnon the son of David loved her."
2 Samuel 13:1

Seduction, Sexual Abuse and Shame

When I first learned of the account of Tamar, I was floored to know that a story this salacious and scandalous was documented in the Bible! Tamar was beautiful. She was the daughter of David (of the famed David and Bathsheba story) and Maacah, a Princess from the neighboring Kingdom of Geshur. Her parents' union was not the best foundation, as Maacah, when they married, became part of David's harem. Maacah's firstborn, a son, Absalom, was David's third son; next was their girl Tamar. By all accounts, Tamar was honored and so loved by her father King David. When the story of Tamar is told, it seems she has just entered puberty; innocent, morals intact, a virgin, trusting and unfortunately, a target. You see, like many of us, the dysfunction in Tamar's family continued from her parents to the next generation. Her brother Absalom was very much like his father; strong-willed and led many times by his masculinity and not his maturity. Her older half-brother Amnon, like his father, too, was led by his lust and not his loyalty. The fallout for Tamar was dreadful. As they grew, Amnon developed quite "a thing" for his little half-sister. The Bible says that Amnon said, *"I'm in love with Tamar, my brother Absalom's sister."* The best description would be that he became completely obsessed with her. His lust, as we will see, had become uncontrollable, which had nothing to do with love. The wickedness in his heart and mind was about to manifest in a whirlwind of seduction, sexual abuse, and shame; for Tamar, the vulnerable. As the account continues, the nefarious plan is put into action; fueled by one Jonadab, a "friend" who outlined to Amnon the specifics of what the plan should entail. Read 2 Samuel 13:5.

There are so many "red flags" in this request! I don't know the culture of that time, but it seems a bit weird for a brother, or even a half-brother, to request to watch his sister prepare food, let alone eat from her hand. By granting Amnon's request, Tamar's father David, unwittingly, and because of his lack of discernment, had become an accomplice to his son's depravity as well as his daughter's disgrace. As Tamar entered Amnon's house, in obedience to her father, and no doubt, care and concern for Amnon, she had no idea of the trap that was set for her. She prepared the food, but he refused to eat. He sent everyone else away, then requested that she move deeper into the deception, into his personal chambers. There the beguilement led to a crescendo. As Tamar moved closer to Amnon to feed him, he grabbed her and made his true intentions known. *"Come to bed with me, my sister"* 2 Samuel 13:11. Tamar was blindsided. She begged and pleaded with him not to dishonor himself, or her; but he refused to listen. Amnon overpowered her, and raped her. Every time I think of how she must have felt, I have to pause and breathe. As terrible as the assault was of her body, her pain was compounded by what happened next.

"Then Amnon hated her with intense hatred. In fact, he hated her more than he had loved her. Amnon said to her, "Get up and get out". "No!" she said to him. "Sending me away would be a greater wrong than what you have already done to me" 2 Samuel 13:15-16.

He didn't listen. Now, for sure, the pain had saturated her soul. The barrage of trouble that followed this whole catastrophe was overwhelming. Tamar was broken and devastated. Absalom was full of rage. Amnon was murdered by Absalom for the revenge of Tamar's rape. David was mourning it all. There is so much to be learned from this tragic tale of family sin and dysfunction. Here are three truths to consider.

Generational Sin Must Be Addressed

One of the most difficult things in life is understanding the weight we carry, of the choices of those who have gone before us. The blessings don't seem heavy at all; it's the inherited sins that burden, blindside, and baffle us. It seems unreasonable, unfair, maybe even incomprehensible at times. It's at these times that we truly have to "settle in" on the Truth of God's Word and ask Him to help us make sense of it all. Tamar, in her innocence, had every reason to believe her life would be a fairy tale. Her Dad was King, her Mom, Princess; to be a "Golden Child" was not far-fetched. Yet there were shadows lurking of generational sins probably unknown to her, that would affect her for the rest of her life. Even though David is described in (1 Samuel 13:14) as a "man after God's own heart," it doesn't negate the fact that he was a sinner. If we just take his most infamous sin with Bathsheba, we'll find that it was not just the act that was so heinous, but his heart concerning his choices. Here is how David's sin unfolded... and how it showed up again in his children; and wrecked the life of one of them, Tamar.

1. **Covetousness** (Exodus 20:17)

Very simply stated, David wanted something/someone that was not his; he wanted another man's wife. He did not stop until he got what he wanted (2 Samuel 11: 2-3). Amnon, like his father, was covetous. Tamar was his sister. She was not his wife. He did not stop until he got what he wanted.

2. **Adultery** (Exodus 20:14)

David committed adultery with Bathsheba. David's sexual sin was passed down to Amnon. It didn't show up in the form of adultery, but it magnified in him in the form of rape.

3. **Murder** (Exodus 20:13)

By proxy, David committed the murder of Uriah, Bathsheba's husband. Absalom murdered his brother to avenge the rape of Tamar.

4. **False Testimony** (Exodus 20:16)

The plot thickened when David schemed to have Uriah come out of combat to sleep with his wife; to cover up his sin. Amnon deceived everyone, including himself. His feelings for Tamar was not love after all, but a plan conceived in lust that brought forth death.

Giants Fall and Giants Fail

It's a wonderful thing when women feel love and protection from their fathers. I'm sure this was the case with Tamar. She just didn't have a "Dad"... her father was King! No doubt she'd heard the story of when he slayed Goliath. Her father made giants fall! Moreover, Biblical history relates that out of nineteen children (twenty including the son that died), Tamar is the only girl mentioned! Can you imagine how she must have been the quintessential Daddy's girl? In her eyes, he was strong but gentle, wise but playful, her provider, her protector.

In Tamar's life, as in many of our lives; our hero, the one who slayed the giant, becomes our giant! But, oftentimes, here's the hard truth. Giants fall. Giants fail. Her father, the one who made giants fall, was her giant who made an epic fail. Did she wonder when he made the request for her to take care of Amnon if it was a wise request? Perhaps it was when Amnon grabbed her, it crossed her mind that her father was at least mistaken. Undoubtedly, as the rape was occurring, her mind was racing. Where is my father? How could he let this happen? We know that her father was foremost in her mind when she began to experience the trauma. Read 2 Samuel 13:13. The wide-eyed innocence of a young girl whose father was her giant. The disappointment of a violated girl whose expectations of protection were shattered in moments; her father nowhere to be found. Giants fall. Giants fail. In all of our lives.

God Wants Us to Operate In Power

Tamar is a tragic Biblical account of epic proportions. There is so much to learn from it as women. I believe the purpose of this story is to encourage us to seek a life that is opposite of what Tamar, due to no fault of her own, had to endure. Here are a few thoughts. Our earthly father may have abused or abandoned us; or had no awareness of how to provide for or protect us, but Our Heavenly Father will never leave us or forsake us (Hebrews 13:5).

Innocence and purity is beautiful and supported in the safety of true Spirit-filled Godly men and women; and that must be discerned. We must not forget the enemy will come to steal, kill, and destroy (John 10:10). Unfortunately, even family may disappoint us in diabolical ways. God has a remedy for that loneliness. God places the lonely in families (Psalm 68:6). Sexual sin permeates your soul; however, it is encountered. The consequences are far more reaching than those directly involved (Leviticus 19:29). Sexual sin infuses people with shame. Shame is a cancer that affects your health, your happiness, your future, your destiny. The only cure for the darkness of shame is to allow the light of Love and Truth to dispel it (Psalm 34:5). Finally, the greatest lesson learned from the innocence of Tamar is that we need power. I don't mean "feminist" power. I mean the power that comes from the knowledge of how precious and powerful and strong we are as a beautiful creation of God! Yes, we need to know His Love. Yes, we need to know our identity. Yes, we need to know we are His. All that needs to be encompassed by His Power! I can prove it!

Remember the Woman with the Issue of Blood in Mark 5? The Bible says she was bleeding for twelve years. Twelve is the number of foundations. This means this was not just a circumstance or an event, it was the foundation of her life. Much like Tamar, whose very existence in her family meant she was subject to endure trauma. When the Woman with the Issue of Blood touched the hem of Jesus' garment, the Bible doesn't say "healing" flowed out of Him. It doesn't say "love" flowed out of Him. The Bible says, "Power" flowed out of Him toward her. Power encompasses love and healing! He doesn't want us to be broken and powerless. He wants us to stand in the knowledge that HE is our Father and what He has done for us! Beyond that, out of all the women in the Bible, the woman caught in adultery, the woman at the well; this woman, whose life was a life of fear and bleeding and pain and anemia and rejection. This woman was the only one Jesus called a daughter. *"Daughter, your faith has made you whole"* Mark 5:34.

To all the daughters, the broken, the Tamars; be healed in Jesus' Name! Reclaim your position as valuable, worthy, beautiful! No matter what the abuse, the abandonment, the pain that you've endured, the Word says you are flawless! *"You are altogether beautiful, my darling; there is no flaw in you"* Song of Solomon 4:7.

Receive His Word, His forgiveness, His healing, His love and His blessings today.

Persis

Darla M. Wright, *46 years old*

"Greet Tryphena and Tryphosa, who have labored in the Lord.
Greet the beloved Persis, who labored much in the Lord."
Romans 16:2

The sun has escaped the horizon and the stars have made a twilight appearance in the night sky–another day of serving the Lord is complete. A new day will greet the beloved Persis soon and many tasks await her servant heart and her wearisome body. She pulls a rickety chair away from her table and rests her creaking bones as she attempts to refuel by filling her stomach with a pinch of bread and a warm broth soup. In the stillness of her dwelling, the light from the lamp on the table dances across the room as the flame weakens and the oil diminishes to nearly nothing. A deep yawn coupled with an exhausted exhale charges her with a short burst of energy for one final task before she expires for the evening. Forcefully lifting her body from a position of rest, spending the very last ounce of energy left within her, she makes her way across the room to retrieve her bottle of oil used to refuel her lamp for the watchful night hours.

The lamp has been refilled, but Persis is running on empty. As she completes this last chore for the day and finally allows herself to put her body to rest for the night, her mind races back to her first task of the day

making a mental checklist of all her daily accomplishments then immediately shifts her thoughts to what tasks await her tomorrow.

Inhale. Exhale. Inhale. Exhale. The room darkens completely as her
eyelids yield to the weight of exhaustion.

Very little is known about Persis, but what we can gather from the
scripture passage in Romans Chapter 16 of Paul's greetings to those who
faithfully served the Lord, is that Persis was not only a servant of the
Lord and beloved by Paul, but she was also a Persian woman among the
Jewish men and woman whom she served alongside. In 515 B.C.,
Esther, also known as Hadassah, was a Jew who lived among the
Persians and became Queen of Persia. During the time of the birth of the
Church, Persis, a Persian woman, served the Church and the Lord
alongside the Jews. Now, this is what I call flipping the script! Esther
had to find favor with the king in order to be chosen as queen. Persis, on
the other hand, did not need to seek the approval of anyone, or did she?
Perhaps Persis, being a Persian woman, serving among the Jews due to
her ethnicity, was compelled to work tirelessly serving the Lord simply
because she truly loved the Lord, *and* felt the need to gain the approval
of those whom she labored with and served alongside. Perhaps she was
not trying to seek approval, but rather freedom?

It is quite possible that Persis lived and breathed the words of
Ephesians 9:10 because of her uncompromising service and devotion to
the Lord. *"Whatever your hand finds to do, do it with your might; for
there is no work or device or knowledge or wisdom in the grave where
you are going."*

What I choose to believe is that Persis truly loved the Lord and the
Church with a true heart to serve and she gave one-hundred percent of
her life to the cause of Christ. However, I do wonder if Persis initially
came to Rome as a slave before getting connected with the Church in
Corinth. Did she serve the Church freely and yet faithfully labored while
still being enslaved by her past? Quite honestly, I do not know and
cannot speak for Persis; however, I can speak for myself and will do so
with an open and honest heart.

Serving is one of my greatest joys, but I have not always served with pure intentions. Please let me explain. God designed me with a servant's heart–it is interwoven into my DNA to serve and I would not want it any other way. However, God had to walk me through a difficult journey of healing, so that I could learn how to serve Him and others with a pure and humble heart. Having a servant heart and a broken heart at the same time created a way of escape for me. The busyness distracted me from addressing the brokenness and the brokenness fueled my pursuit to continually seek the approval I longed to receive from my father. Thus creating a vicious cycle of perpetual rejection and a very skewed understanding of what it meant to truly labor for the Lord. I was serving, but was serving in bondage–seeking approval from the wrong father.

On the night of my 38th birthday, while sitting down with my family for a dinner out, robust voices and laughter filled the room along with the clanking of dishes and the chiming ring of silverware repeatedly touching the stoneware dishes so much so that I barely heard my phone ring. I answered, and on the other end of that call was the deep trembling voice of my older brother informing me that my dad had just gone into cardiac arrest and was rushed into ICU. By the miraculous grace of God, my father recovered enough to be released from the hospital. One evening before he was discharged, I went to the hospital to pay my dad a visit. My older sibling was leaving as I was walking in the door; I heard my brother tell my dad that he loved him and my dad echoed back, "I love you." I was in total shock to hear my dad speak *those* three words. My parents were not affectionate or affirming at all–no hugs, no kisses, no words of affirmation were given, nor were the words, 'I love you' ever spoken. I vividly remember standing at the foot of my dad's hospital bed when a wave of confidence rushed over me. My thoughts were so loud in my head it was as if they were spoken aloud. "Maybe dad will tell me he loves me too," I thought.

As we were preparing to leave, I leaned in close to the bed where my father was sitting upright and fully awake. I sensed my time with him was short and I wanted him to know that I loved him, hoping this moment would be different, that he would express his love for me as well in return. I said, "I love you, Dad," and he said nothing. His response was void of the affirmation of his love I had hoped to hear. My heart felt like it broke into a million pieces. The words 'I love you' were, in fact, the last words I heard my father speak, but they were not spoken to me. His silence shattered my identity and my heart felt betrayed. How could my own father withhold his love from me? I fought back every tear that welled up in my eyes as we made our way back to our car. Sinking down into the passenger seat, I quietly fastened my seatbelt and fixed my gaze out the window staring off into the night sky as a flood of tears endlessly streamed down my face. Yet again, I felt unloved, unwanted and unworthy of being loved.

On September 8th, 2015, my father passed into eternity. I love him and miss him so very much and I do truly believe he loved me; he just did not know how to say it or show it. The following year, I had three separate encounters with the Lord. Each encounter brought healing to my wounded heart. In one of these specific encounters, Jesus, hand in hand, led me into an art museum and upon a wall where we turned and faced, there were three hanging murals of me as a child portraying three extremely painful memories. Below each framed memory were name plates with an inscription for each mural–UNWANTED, UNWORTHY, UNLOVED. Still holding my hand, He led me through a wall into a room full of the brightest light I have ever seen radiating out from the cross standing upright in the room. As we walked around the cross, the light diminished and I could see a gruesome bloodbath on the back side of the cross. I had to look away. I fixed my eyes on Jesus to avoid seeing all of that blood. He stooped down and grabbed a small bucket and brush and He led me back into the room where the painful memories of these murals were mocking me. Jesus not only wanted me to exchange the lies of the enemy for His truth, but He also wanted to restore my identity. With my eyes blurred and my face stained with tears, I saw Jesus in a long white flowing robe dip the paintbrush into a bucket of His blood and He painted over the letters UN on each nameplate until each mural read: WANTED, WORTHY, LOVED. He put down the bucket and brush, and then gracefully wrapped His arms around me and tenderly spoke over me as He held me in His embrace— *"be loved, my beloved, be loved, my beloved, be loved..."*

When I opened my eyes, I knew I had been with the Lord and He had restored and redeemed me in an instant. I had ***allowed*** a lifetime of pain and rejection to define my identity and from that broken place, I tried to love and serve the Lord and others. I have since learned that the

One who calls you is the one who also keeps you. God has been faithful to teach me how to labor joyfully, love sacrificially, and serve with humility and in obedience. However, I have learned, too, that there is a responsibility that God requires of us in order to keep our freedom. We must stand firm, defend the freedom Christ purchased, and **not allow** ourselves to become enslaved again to sin. Galatians 5:1-3 reads, *"It is for freedom that Christ has set us free. Stand firm, then, and do not let yourselves be burdened again by a yoke of slavery."*

As I read the passage in Romans introducing Persis, it stood out to me that Paul did not just address Persis as one who labored much in the Lord, but rather, he addressed her as the beloved Persis who labored much in the Lord. As I sought the Lord while I studied this woman, God reminded me of the encounter I just shared with you where He called out the beloved in me because I could not see it within me. As I was praying I heard God ask, "Was Persis much different than you?" Paul obviously loved Persis and he recognized her faithfulness to the Lord and the Church in her serving, but was Paul also calling out the beloved in Persis like Jesus called it out in me? Was Persis so busy and weary from her laboring that she found a way to escape the murals of her own past? How about you? Do you need the beloved called out in you? It is my most greatest honor to serve and labor for the LORD and it is my second greatest honor to love people—assuring them they are loved, wanted, and worthy of being loved by our Heavenly Father.

In closing, would you, for a moment, examine your hands and your heart? How do they labor? Who do they serve? Are they tired and weary? I know of two hands and one heart that labored greatly in love, costing Him everything, which was the joy that was set before Him. Jesus paid the ultimate price to reconcile you to your Heavenly Father. No need to seek His approval—you already have it! You are LOVED. You are WANTED. You are WORTHY of being loved and forgiven because of the blood of Jesus Christ. In all of your doing, do it unto the Lord.

"Let us not become weary in doing good, for at the proper time we will reap a harvest if we do not give up. Therefore, as we have opportunity, let us do good to all people, especially to those who belong to the family of believers" Galatians 6:9-10.

Hagar

Lynda McLeod Smith, *74 years young*

"Now Sarai, Abram's wife, had borne him no children. And she had an Egyptian maidservant whose name was Hagar." Genesis 16:1

One of my favorite video's is titled: "The God who Sees." It was filmed in Israel and is only eleven minutes long, but very impactful. It is written by Kathie Lee Gifford and Nicole C. Mullen. It speaks concerning the life of Hagar. We're not certain Hagar had all the emotions sung in the song above, but probably most of them. Many of us have experienced desert times in our lives and felt God was nowhere to be found just like Hagar, but then we see in one way or another, at the end of our trial, He was there all the time.

"But I am poor and needy; yet the Lord thinks upon me. You are my help and my deliverer, do not delay, O my God" Psalm 40:17.

There was a time in my own personal life that I entered a horrendous wilderness/desert. I came home from work one evening and before I had gotten out of the car, my dad met me and told me to go pack my things and get out, he had raised me long enough. I was nineteen. Because I grew up in a very dysfunctional home, I was insecure, fearful, and vulnerable and soon realized I was easy prey for victimizers. One evening, a man attacked me with the intent to rape me. I fought back and he kicked me out of a moving car and drove off. As I settled my emotions after I hit the ground and looked around, I realized I was sitting in the middle of a field with a dirt road running through it. My last remembered thought was, "I wonder how I'll find my car which was in a different location, and get myself home." I had no other memories until I woke up the next morning in my parents' home (not my apartment) and my car was sitting outside where I had always parked it. After I became a follower of Christ Jesus, the Lord informed me my *Angel* had gotten both myself and my car home that night. Amazing!

"Therefore, behold I will allure her, will bring her into the wilderness, and speak comfort to her. I will give her, her vineyards from there, and the valley of Achor (trouble) as a door of hope..." Hosea 2:14-15.

Hagar had a difficult home life just as I had. She was treated harshly, she was devalued as a person, and basically expendable, just as my life had been. Hagar actually took two trips to the desert. Her first (Genesis 16:6), she left by her own choosing; she was fed up with being mistreated. But when told to go home by the Angel, she obeyed. The 2nd time (Genesis 21:10), she was forced to leave and this time, God moved her and her son to a new location to live their own lives, never to return to her past life again. It was over!

When I look at my life and compare it to Hagar, I see some similarities. I was forced to pack and leave home alone at nineteen. While at home, I was treated harshly as well. But after leaving, I soon realized I didn't have to put up with mistreatment like I was forced to do while living at home. In fact, a number of times through the years, when others tried to mistreat me, I physically packed my things and left, because I could, and I would never go back.

After being kicked out of the car, I didn't have the privilege of seeing the Angel who rescued me, but Hagar did. Here is her response:

"Then she called the name of the Lord who spoke to her, You-are-the-God-who-sees; for she said, "Have I also here seen Him who sees me?" Genesis 16:13.

HAGAR

In my 25th year of life, I went through multiple tragedies: cancer, loss of my ability to ever have children, betrayal, loss of house and home, depression, rape and then became homeless, with no one who would help me; I lived off the fruit of the trees that grew around me. Walking through these tragedies was difficult but at the end of that season, I came to know Christ as my personal Savior and realized that all these things really had worked out for my good. God had brought me to the end of myself and it was there that Jesus was waiting for me. People often devalue what God holds dear.

"And we know that all things work together for good to those who love God, to those who are the called according to His purpose" Romans 8:28.

Hagar was alone and trapped with nowhere to turn. When she felt the end of her life had to be near, (provisions had run out), God stepped in and the Angel of the Lord appeared and said to her in Genesis 16:10: *"I will multiply your descendants exceedingly, so that they shall not be counted for multitude and I will make you a great nation."* Can you imagine Hagar's response after a lifetime of rejection, being unfairly treated, desertion, and being cut off with very little provision? In Genesis 21, the Lord intervened with spiritual (v18) and physical (v19) provision.

Looking at Hagar's life span:
- Her past: Possible rejection by her own family; servant in Egypt; she was given to strangers and taken from Egypt to another land.
- Her present: She was forced to go alone into the desert, with little provision, and it was very possible she could die there.
- And then an Angel from God says to her: God will multiply your descendants exceedingly—you can't even count the multitude of them; and I will make you a great nation (you will survive and thrive).

We think the world can dictate our future. That they can take us into bondage, and enslave us somehow, when God has bigger and better plans for us. Hagar had a future like nothing she could have imagined, and the God of all Creation sent His Angel to tell her the truth about it. When I look at my own life today, God has been amazingly good to me and His prophetic words to me about my future are far from what my past would reflect my life would become.

> "We think sometimes that poverty is only being
> hungry, naked, and homeless.
> The poverty of being unwanted, unloved,
> and uncared for is the greatest poverty."
> **Mother Teresa**

"Your eye saw my substance, being yet unformed, and in Your book they all were written, the days fashioned for me, when as yet there were none of them" Psalm 139:16.

***

"For I know the thoughts that I think towards you, says the Lord, Thoughts of peace and not of evil, To give you a future and a hope" Jeremiah 29:11.

God's greatest promotions are for those who have traversed the desert well, listening for His voice and obedient.

Devotional 39

Michal

Ashlyn Pinner, *31 years old*

"Now Michal, Saul's daughter, loved David. And they told Saul, and the thing pleased him." 1 Samuel 18:20

T he woman who ridiculed her husband's worship. The woman who mocked David as he danced before the Lord. I used to criticize her. *How could she? How dare she?* I now have compassion for her. I see myself in her. I understand her.

We are first introduced to Michal in the shadows of her father, Saul, in 1 Samuel 14. Saul was in the middle of his downfall, determined to put David to death. Saul's oldest daughter, Merab, was the first option for David, but plans changed and she married Adriel. Meanwhile, Michal announced her love for David. Saul seized the opportunity to gain control over David and decided to use Michal as a pawn in his battle plan.

In 1 Samuel 18, Saul worked up the plan: *"I will give her to him so that she may be a snare to him and so that the hand of the Philistines may be against him."* In order for David to marry Michal, he had to defeat an army of Philistines. A mission that no average man would be able to accomplish, yet David was victorious. This is where we see Saul's hatred and Michal's hurts dig deep.

Michal was married, although she was the second option. Her father hated her husband and sought to kill him. She was used like a chess piece. Not good enough. Less than. Rejected. Used. Manipulated. Sound familiar? Fast forward and Michal used collected idols as tools in her deception. She lied, took total control, and watched her marriage deteriorate. The more I read Michal's story, the more I understood her bitterness and offense. Yes, she was the woman who mocked David's worship in 2 Samuel. But first, she was the girl who was hurt and offended.

I have been the woman who has spewed hateful comments. The woman who seethes with jealousy and pride. The woman who masks insecurity with ugly. But first, I was the little girl afraid of rejection. I look back on my story and see the moments of hurt that compacted into bitterness. Rejection from my supposed friend group in middle school. Manipulation in high school dating relationships. Walking through family divorces and division. Feelings of insecurity and inferiority. Prideful church hurt. Instead of healing, I allowed my feelings to roll into offense. I can pinpoint the time when I realized how far I had let my feelings take me. I call it my *La Cantina Conviction.*

Nearly five years ago, I sat across from my boyfriend-turned-husband and said four of the most hateful, ugly words: I don't need you. They were coated with attitude and delivered with a tone of rebellion. I repeated it and reworded it, making sure he understood. I assured him that I didn't count on him. I didn't rely on him. I could provide and decide. I could survive and thrive, with or without him. I sound like a lovely dinner date, right? I had let unhealed feelings and fear of rejection become ugly offense.

After years of compounding hurt, I turned to prideful mocking. I protected my heart by putting up walls. I was Michal. Past rejection tainted my view of love and submission. Thankfully, my ever-patient husband kept pursuing, providing, and protecting while God began convicting, and correcting. Through prayer, reading the Word, and some needed humbling, God dug into the dusty parts of my heart, cleaning out baggage that weighed heavily on my heart. I learned to let the Lord's love in. I realized that to fully heal, I had to first fully trust. As the Lord walked me to freedom, I learned the beauty and biblical value of surrender, submission, and celebration.

For so long, I fought my own battles. I resisted His assistance. I confused surrender with failure. I believed that I had to do it all, be it all, and handle it all. It wasn't until I gave way to His authority over my life that I experienced His full love, forgiveness, and freedom. Surrender is an outward expression of our trust in God. Surrender is the end of selfishness and resistance. Surrender is giving in. Do I trust God's Word? Do I believe He is in control? Do I have faith in His love for me? Then, comes submission. Submission has been debated, tainted, and ridiculed in our society. Submission is often seen as weakness and ignorant obedience. Submission is so much more. It is the decision to *acknowledge and obey treatment, or influence.*

As I gave way to God's influence, He renewed my mind and heart. God turned my fear of rejection into confident submission. The more humble I grew, the more I saw my husband's leadership. I started to see my husband the way God created him. I realized his role in my life: leader, protector, helper.

Reflecting on the rewards of my healing, I can't help but wonder how different Michal's story could have been. Her pride prevented God from being God. Her idols and offense interfered with her obedience. What if she would have had a moment of total surrender? What if she would have submitted her hurt and heart to God? Would she have been dancing alongside David in worship? What would she have been assigned to accomplish for God?

God's continual work in my life reminds me of how far He has brought me. I am thankful for the pain and rejection of my past that led me straight to Him. I am grateful for the offense and fear that forced me to seek His freedom. I stand and celebrate. I sing and dance before the Lord. Because He set me free.

What is it that you need healing from? What is that deep hurt you are hiding? What has grown into offense? Will you surrender it to the Lord today?

Surrender and submission are the first steps of a life on fire. A life that chases after God and the calling on your life. Offense will extinguish that fire. Humility ignites it.

"As the ark of the Lord was entering the City of David, Michal daughter of Saul watched from a window. And when she saw King David leaping and dancing before the Lord, she despised him in her heart" 2 Samuel 6:16.

God is after your heart. He wants to heal it and set you free. He wants you to love fully and wholly. He wants you to dance before Him.

The Widow

of Zarephath

Apostle Wilma Berry, *63 years young*

"So he arose and went to Zarephath. And when he came to the gate
of the city, indeed a widow was there gathering sticks. And he called to her
and said, "Please bring me a little water in a cup, that I may drink."
1 Kings 17:10

The faith of the widow... Wow! It's awesome when God speaks to the prophet about His plan to use our lives. Many of us have received prophetic words; sometimes, it's in three days or in thirty days, this or that will happen. Many prophetic words have no definite arrival time attached to them. Many times, we hear the word of the Lord and we are enamored with that word, we're expectant of that word. We are sometimes even confused by prophetic words we have received. But praise be unto God! Receiving a word from the Lord causes us to have Hope. The Widow of Zarephath had **HER** plan. She woke up that morning with **HER** plan.

- Take this little bit of meal that I have and make a cake.
- Feed my son.
- Then die.

Normally, most people awaken from a night's sleep and don't have the plan to die. We instead want to live. Work on our goals, accomplish our 'to-do-list,' go shopping, you know, maybe have some fun. But this particular widow woman woke up that morning with a different plan. And when the prophet of the Lord—Elijah came, he totally shattered her plan. He pushed her plan to the side and he said *this is what the Lord has said*. When the man of God said there will be no rain... God's plan was already made. God already knew where the resources would come from. God already had a plan of sustenance, a plan of care for his servant. Beloved... God already has a plan for our lives to get the Victory! God's plan is a definite word and in this instance, it's an immediate word. I just love it that the widow woman's plan was totally preempted by the plan of the Lord. As the man of God said, first make me a little cake and bring a cup of water. Because the Lord says, *"The meal and the oil shall not run out, until the rain returns."* Hallelujah. Thank You, Jesus.

The widow's encounter with the prophet ... What I love is when the widow encountered Elijah, she didn't have doubts. She had some concerns, but she didn't have doubts. She ran on to make the cake and to get the water for the man of God. And that was the beginning of a long period of time, because we know that the rain didn't return for a number of years. They were together breaking bread. In the Jewish culture, they don't cut the bread; instead, they break the bread. So they were, in a sense, foreshadowing communion. This is supernatural provision, as the bread is coming from a jar that the Lord Himself is replenishing. Can you imagine going into your kitchen... and the flower, the rice, the pasta, whatever it is that you like, the Lord Himself is replenishing that grain in your container. The oils of today everybody wants to use, all the good oils, are avocado oil, olive oil, and grapeseed oil, all these various oils to cook with. We want to have the most healthy oil, to make the most healthy dishes for our families. Miraculously, the Lord replenished that oil and I would say, in my Holy Ghost imagination, that was probably the purest oil to cook with to make these little cakes. God has such a sense of humor, He is a long term planner.

The Lord, through the power of the Holy Spirit, spoke through Elijah, God's Prophet, for that season. He already had the plan. You go to the brook. The ravens are going to feed you. You're going to drink from that particular brook. But the next part of the plan? I already have a widow woman in Zarephath who will... make a way, make provision for you. We'll take care of your daily needs. God is awesome friends, because He knows what we need. God has already prepared the blessings for us. He's already blessed us with every blessing that pertains to life and godliness. *It's so exciting for us as believers to know that we are operating in a finished work.* That God has already called us. He has chosen us. He has made this great plan for us. He's accepted us in the Beloved! God came to the widow... the man of God is sent to her and to her alone in the city of Sidon. Read Luke 4:24-26.

God has a way of making us know that He sees us, He hears us, even in our desperation, and He answers us. He answers right on time! This was not at all normal. This was an instant prophecy. After the rejoicing begins to be routine, at least three years, this miracle provision period of time, look what happens. Tragedy comes to the widow's house. If you're like me when my husband went to Heaven in 2021, I felt like a tragedy had come to my home. I questioned myself, did I pray enough? Did I say I love you enough?... once I calmed down, I allowed God's peace to overflow within me. Then, I realized I had done everything that God wanted and I was Fred's *God sent* wife. I remembered Fred's words that I was his first wife and his only wife! To God be the Glory! We have been together for twenty-eight years! Amen!

The results of the widow's perseverance ... There is a transition in the relationship between Elijah and the widow woman. I love that after eating with people, you do get closer to them. You also have a desire to give and support each other. So, after she's given, after she serves him, and after she makes a place for the man of God in her home, there is a familiar bond that develops. Body of Christ, we are family! The widow woman responded and she went and did according to the saying of Elijah. She and he and her house did eat for many days. Now, they talk about the widow, they talk about her son, but here they say, *and her house did eat many days*. It doesn't say exactly if there's anybody else in the house, other than Elijah. The widow's house became a storehouse. Her house became a treasure house of the things that were needed in that hour. Meal and oil, so much that they were sustained for many days. Read 1 Kings 17:17-24.

Now this widow woman, she's been months and years experiencing miraculous meals, miraculous oil, but her son's sickness was her litmus test. When her son died, she said, "Oh my God, you came here... I thought it was a blessing, but now you're just poking your finger at my sins. Now, in a sense, you brought trouble to my house." So, she totally forgot that she's been eating good, cooking well. The whole house has been nourished and sustained, so why something so close to her heart? Her child is seemingly being taken away, but in reality this test will show forth the glory of God. The other thing that's extremely surprising, if you know you didn't put any extra flour in a jar and the jar keeps filling up, that's a miracle. But once she sees her son raised, she says now... *I really believe you are a true man of God*. It's so interesting that we trust the things that we see. And sometimes, we take for granted the miracles of God, the small miracles, the daily miracles, the things that impact our daily lives. It's a miracle for us to get up. It's a miracle for us to be able to use our limbs. It's a miracle for us to be in our right minds. It's a miracle for us to recognize that Jesus Christ is our elder brother and our Lord and our Savior. All these things are miracles. But sometimes, we wait for something really big to say, "Oh my God, you must be a true man of God. You must be speaking the Word of the Lord."

The state or season of widowhood ... Widowhood, the desperation of the season that had just passed, the season of her husband being lost, the season of her being alone. The season of her having to make a living to take care of the entire household. The season of her having to nurture that child. It doesn't say how long she was alone with her child, or the year that the husband passed away. I personally know from the last two years, the season of widowhood is exceptionally complex. It's difficult. It's challenging. It's lonely. It's frustrating. But remember, we have a better covenant, so I have this hope in me because I know with certainty, I know beyond any doubts, where my husband is. And so the joy of the Lord comes to me, stays with me, and sustains me. I recognize the sovereignty of God, that He is God and He is faithful. And so I trust in the faithfulness and the trustworthiness of God to sustain me. During that time, she did not have the same covenant. Then, if they were good people, they would go into the bosom of Abraham. Scripture doesn't really talk about that. It talks about her being a widow and the struggles of widowhood. It's a season of transition. It's a season of having to make a whole lot of decisions in a short period of time and then to wonder, did I make the right decision? So, we can relate. I can personally relate to the widow.

THE WIDOW of Zarephath

Reality check, being a widow... You know, we all need a little reality check at times. In the scriptures, it says if the widow is less than thirty years old or so and doesn't have children, she should be returned to her father's house. That's the Old Testament we know, right? We are always all considered the Bride of Christ. So, even if we get married as a female, we are still the Bride of Christ. I did ponder this before I was married. I was really learning and leaning into the fact that Jesus Christ is my husband. I strongly desired to learn how to be a wife. I learned and came to understand how the Lord courts us and how to abide with Him. And that strength in my Christian walk helped me really learn how to be a wife. After Fred's passing, I looked again at these scriptures: Isaiah 54:4-8 KJV: *"Fear not; for thou shalt not be ashamed: neither be thou confounded; for thou shalt not be put to shame: for thou shalt forget the shame of thy youth, and shalt not remember the reproach of thy widowhood any more. For thy Maker is thine husband; the LORD of hosts is his name; and thy Redeemer the Holy One of Israel; The God of the whole earth shall he be called. For the LORD hath called thee as a woman forsaken and grieved in spirit, and a wife of youth, when thou wast refused, saith thy God. For a small moment have I forsaken thee; but with great mercies will I gather thee. In a little wrath I hid my face from thee for a moment; but with everlasting kindness will I have mercy on thee, saith the LORD thy Redeemer."*

The Bible says the Lord is my husband and He cares for me. And so we have to take comfort in the Word of God. We must stay encouraged, to stand on the Word of God. To know that the Lord Himself is so good to us, so faithful to us, that whatever we're going through, He already knows about it, and He already has a plan for us. Even though it seems like, *Oh my God, why...?* The *whys* can't necessarily be answered in this Earth realm. There are mysteries in God. There are things that we're not going to know on this side. God is God and God is sovereign. That's just the name of that tune, really! There are just some things we have to accept, some things we're not going to know in this earthly plane. But we're called to come up higher, to be in the Spirit and to fellowship in the Spirit, so we can receive the comfort of the Spirit. When we get to Heaven, we can ask some questions, worship our Lord, run around, and be happy there and see all that we can see there. Amen!

~In Loving Memory of Apostle Fred Berry, Azusa Street Mission (2021)

Meet the Author

Deborah G. Hunter is a wife, mother, author, inspiration-
al speaker, philanthropist, and CEO & Publisher of Hunter
Heart Publishing and co-owner of Hunter Entertainment
Network. She has written eleven books of her own, including
her bestselling book *Holy Spirit, the Promise Left for the Believer* and
has ghostwritten dozens of books for people all over the world. Deborah
travels nationally and internationally on her mission to "Offer God's
Heart to a Dying World" through the inspired gift of writing, personal
testimony, mentorship, and prophetic counseling of spiritual leaders all
over the world. She serves as an avid philanthropist through her charity,
Stir Up the Gift, dedicated to providing support for the needy around the
world, including the country of Japan after the wake of the 2011 Earth-
quake/Tsunami that ravaged this country.

Deborah has been a born-again believer since the age of twelve. She
was ordained as a Minister in Prophetic Gifting on July 7, 2007, in
Kitzingen, Germany from International Gospel Church. She received her
Bachelor of Arts Degree in Biblical Studies/Theology from *Minnesota
Graduate School of Theology*, Magna Cum Laude. She is the Colorado
State Director for the *Prayer Council of the USA* and is Spiritual Advisor
for the missionary organization *Lion's Light International*.

Deborah is married to Chris Hunter, Jr., radio personality and CEO
of Hunter Entertainment Network, a conglomerate of Christian media
outlets. They share in the raising of their three children together, Jade,
Elijah, and Ja'el, and are the father and stepmother of three, along with
five beautiful grandchildren. They reside in the beautiful mountains of
Colorado.

www.ingramcontent.com/pod-product-compliance
Lightning Source LLC
Chambersburg PA
CBHW011428010726
47494CB00011B/2547